Another Perfect Catastrophe

Also by Brad Barkley

Alison's Automotive Repair Manual
Money, Love
Circle View

Another Perfect Catastrophe

and Other Stories

Brad Barkley

Thomas Dunne Books

St. Martin's Press   ≈   New York

Thomas Dunne Books.
An imprint of St. Martin's Press.

The stories in this collection have appeared, in slightly different form, in the following
publications: "Another Perfect Catastrophe" and "Those Imagined Lives" in *Glimmer
Train;* "The Way It's Lasted" on USATODAY.com; "The Small Machine" in *Book* magazine; "The Properties of Stainless Steel" and "Beneath the Deep, Slow Motion" in the
Virginia Quarterly Review; "Beneath the Deep, Slow Motion" also in *New Stories from
the South: The Year's Best, 2002;* "19 Amenities" and "The Atomic Age" in the *Southern
Review;* "Mistletoe" in *Arts & Letters;* "St. Jimmy" in the *Mid-American Review.*

www.stmartins.com

Design by Phil Mazzone

ISBN 0-312-29147-7

First Edition: March 2004

10 9 8 7 6 5 4 3 2 1

For my parents, with love and thanks

And for Jim Whitehead, in memoriam

Contents

Acknowledgments

Many thanks, as always, to my agent and friend, Peter Steinberg, and to those who cast their eyes and minds on early drafts, especially the beloved Thursday night group—Susan Allen, Jack DuBose, Stephen Dunn, Mary Edgerly, Michael Hughes, Barb Hurd, Kevin Kehrwald, Keith Schlegel, Maggie Smith, and Karen Zealand; also to Susan Perabo, to my friends in West Virginia and Maine, and to the editors of the magazines that first published these stories, particularly Staige Blackford, Michael Griffith, and Susan Burmeister-Brown and Linda Swanson-Davies. Thanks to George Singleton just because, and to Fred Chappell for too many reasons to mention.

Thanks to my friend and editor, Alicia Brooks, who gets it, to Carin Siegfried for grabbing the wheel with grace and humor, and to Stephen Lee, in advance. I am grateful to others at St. Martin's

Acknowledgments

for their continued support and faith: George Witte, editor in chief; John Cunningham, associate publisher; Matthew Shear, vice president and publisher; Kevin Sweeney, production editor; and Michael Storrings, jacket design. And thanks to the incomparable band Firewater, whose great song title I swiped for my own.

Thanks for their support to the Maryland State Arts Council and to Frostburg State University, and to many others who help keep the raft on course in a variety of ways, to friends scattered everywhere, to Lucas and Alex, and to the lovely Mary B.

*If some great catastrophe is not announced every morning,
we feel a certain void. Nothing in the paper today, we sigh.*

—Lord Acton

Another Perfect Catastrophe

The Way It's Lasted

My father insists that because he is dying of cancer, he has every right to drive seven hours south, share my house for as long as he wants, and see firsthand the brand-new Noah's Ark that the Freewill Baptist Church is erecting here. He explains all of this in a long, rambling message to my answering machine.

"Tell Billy I'm coming," he says, pausing. "Let him know to look for me before the cocktail hour." I listen several times to the recording, the way he treats the machine like some reluctant secretary who might, with enough coaxing, relay messages to me. The machine still has that scrap of Laney's voice on it, asking the anonymous world to state its business and the time of day, to wait for the beep. For the last three months, here is my morning routine: eat bran flakes out of a Cool Whip container, watch the morning sideshows on TV, wade through some of the sixty-three comp papers I have, always, to grade, then push the blue button on the machine and listen to Laney's scratchy voice. I tell the empty kitchen that my business is remaining in love with my not-yet-ex-wife, waiting for her to decide that tossing me for her watercolor instructor was the wrong idea. The time is midmorning. I never wait for the beep.

So by five o'clock Thursday Dad has arrived in North Carolina and we are well into the cocktail hour, as he likes to call it, confirming it with quart bottles of St. Pauli Girl. His Corvette, which he bought new for four thousand dollars in 1966, sits ticking and dripping in my driveway. The car is red on red, the fiberglass cracked above the wheel wells, the rest polished and gleaming. My father leans back in the bent-willow chair Laney made, his face and hands their own deep red from driving with the top down, his head shaved and pale in splotches where he tried dabbing on sunscreen. August heat bears down on us, but he sits there with his red satin Pennsylvania Corvette Club jacket zipped up like it's early November. His full name, *Tommy Kesler*, is embossed on the breast pocket, the same as it's painted on the front license plate of the car, a plate he had made for five bucks at some kiosk in the mall.

"You know what?" I say, "You're starting to look like that car." And it's true, the same way spouses come to look like each other, only Dad had the car a year before he married my mother, and has had it still in the six years since she died.

"You mean the wear and tear, the ruin." He looks at me over the newspaper and over his glasses, using both to search for his daily horoscope. "It's true, son, cancer is an awful ravager of a man."

I stare at him a minute, smirking. "Dad, you don't have cancer."

"Billy . . ." He draws down the newspaper. "I know that denial is one of the stages of grief, but you need to move on. I forget what's next, but you can find out. Should be on the Internet somewhere."

"Dad . . ."

"I think it's anger. Maybe . . . I don't know. Hell, whatever suits you."

"How about incredulity?"

He looks at me. "Goddamn English teachers."

We are quiet a while. He turns the pages of the paper while I finish off my beer and toss the empty into the front yard. Out here I have no neighbors, and this little act of lawlessness is something I do, then tell myself it's evidence of how much things have improved since Laney's departure. *Desperado, outlaw, thrower of beer bottles.* The new me. I once washed my socks in a bucket with the garden hose, and when drunk will allow myself to piss in the sink or out the back door, standing on the stoop.

Dad finds his horoscope and tells me that it promises Taurus an emphasis on creativity, advises that he organize his priorities. He says that spending time with me is a priority now, with his "impending death."

"Impending in maybe thirty years," I tell him. "Impending when I'm drawing Social Security." Five years have passed since a few blood tests came back skewed and his doctor mentioned non-Hodgkin's lymphoma in a long list of things it *might* be. Subsequent tests nailed it down as an infection, but after my mother died my father reinvented himself, fully embracing his imagined disease. He read all the books, joined a cancer victim's support group, walked for the cure, shaved his head to look the part. My mother, in her own death, had made the wire services and the nightly news—she was killed by a faulty electric fry pan that shorted out through the handles, and after a six-figure settlement and lawyer fees, I think what my father was left with (besides new carpet for the Vette) was some combination of loneliness and jealousy over the spectacle of her passing. So he created his own. He has been dying for so long now that I can imagine not believing it when it finally does happen.

"Hey, remember these, the paper lanterns?" he says. He pulls together the four corners of the sports page and twists them at the top, then twists the four openings to make a kind of hollow paper boat. "We used to set fire to them over the ball field."

"Yeah, I remember," I tell him. "You almost burned up Mr. Schlegel's lawn mower." All his life my father has set about to amuse me with little stunts of the type that used to be known as parlor tricks. He could balance an egg on its end, pull quarters from his nose, skewer a balloon with toothpicks without popping it. My memory of him is compressed into one or two days' worth of time—he would return noisily from some place or another in the Vette, show me a few tricks at the kitchen table, then rush out the door again, like some hurried magician hired to entertain me in five-minute increments.

"We should do one again," he says. "Like the old times. You know you have an honest-to-God lake across the street? I found it out walking today."

I open another beer and drink. "That's not a lake, Dad, it's a construction runoff pond. And this house is about all I have. I'd rather not burn it down."

He is quiet and we sit and watch the evening lower itself over the house and yard, until the mosquitoes drive us inside. At the kitchen table I mark a good inch of comp papers, just throwing grades at them quickly, while Dad paces around the kitchen and swallows fifteen vitamin C pills, one at a time, with orange juice.

He stops, wipes his mouth with the dish towel. "Billy, what if I told you I had cancer?"

I laugh out loud, having just read the opening of a freshman essay on euthanasia: *Since the beginning of mankind, man has seen many different ways of dealing with the problem of death.*

He nudges me with his forefinger. "Well, what if?"

"Dad, you've been telling the world that for five years now. Why should tonight be any different?"

He has dressed for bed, stripped down to paisley boxers and a T-shirt, still wearing his Corvette jacket and a beeper he never bothers to turn on. "Really this time. What if?"

"Oh, *really* this time," I say, and as the words leave my mouth I see Laney calling me a sarcastic prick just before she threw a wooden spoon at my head. "You're like that children's story, the boy who cried non-Hodgkin's lymphoma," I tell him. "Just drop it."

Dad picks up the salt shaker and balances it on edge. "Hey, we need to head out tomorrow and see that ark," he says. "I want you to come with me."

"It's really nothing to see, believe me."

He rubs his hand over the five o'clock shadow covering his head. He keeps it shaved so that the ladies in Buena Vista where he lives will think he's still having chemo and will bring him chicken dinners. "The story was in our paper, all the way up in

Carlisle. 'Church Rebuilds Noah's Ark,' it said. Cute little sidebar about the drought here, too."

I mark a comma splice, start skimming the rest. "We can go see," I tell him, "but you're in for a letdown."

He nods. "Won't be the first. No sir."

"You had a long drive," I tell him. "You should sleep."

"We should do something, though. We never did all that much, did we, Billy?"

I shrug. "You were an okay father, if that's what you're fishing for. Kids thought it was cool that my dad sold swimming pools. You were entertaining. You didn't do any damage."

"But you say 'were,' not 'are.'" He snaps and unsnaps a button on his Corvette jacket.

"I don't need much fathering, at thirty-one."

"And I guess I never did much, at thirty-one, did I?"

I drag two beers from the fridge and hand him one. "Okay, listen," I tell him, "you're here for however long, we sit around, take in a ball game on TV, drink some beer. I'll take you to see the ark. Then you go home. Let's leave the big, weepy scenes to TV movies, okay? I've had my fill of moroseness for this year."

He sits and drinks, rubs his scalp, nods. "What's the story with you and that girl?"

"*Laney,* Dad. We were married four years. I'd think you'd know her name."

"Well. So what of her?"

I shrug again, looking down at the euthanasia essay, trying to remember if I've read it or not. I decide I have and give it a C plus. *Much improved,* I write. "I guess what of her is that she's in another guy's bed right now. Not much ambiguity there, huh?"

He looks away, frowns at the wall. I toss him a small stack of essays. "Here you go, grade a few. Then you can say we did something together."

He narrows his eyes at me. "What do you mean, Billy? I'm not trained in this."

"Just pick up a pen. Come on, it's fun. Give it a B minus, then write, 'Try a little harder next time.'"

He frowns again, shakes his head. "I didn't raise you like this, to shirk your responsibilities."

"Hey, maybe that's the next stage of grief—shirking."

He lifts the papers and places them back on my stack. "Must be the first stage, then."

"First? You've been dying half a decade now," I say.

"Right," he says and looks at me. "And that girl's been gone three months."

Near two in the morning I hear him moving through the hallways, muttering to himself, opening the refrigerator, clicking the mouse on the computer. He started an online club called the Tommy Kesler Society and so far has tracked down and recruited seventeen Tommy Keslers, two of them women, one of them as far away as Madagascar. They have nothing in common and little to do beyond tracking down the next Tommy Kesler. Some of them plan to meet next year at a Western Sizzlin'.

Again I can't sleep and so lie in the dark looking up at the glow-in-the-dark stars Laney stuck to the ceiling. In college she'd majored in astronomy, because, she said, it was the only area of study where a final exam could be canceled by clouds. On our ceiling she made the Big Dipper, Orion, Cassiopeia, all to scale, saying she didn't want to forget the knowledge she worked so hard to gain, no matter how useless it might be. I reach over to her empty side of the bed, the sheets smooth and cool. One of my old T-shirts is still stashed under the headboard where she kept it in case of a fire, so the firefighters wouldn't see her naked. I pull the shirt to my face and breathe it in, then turn over and pick up the phone. I punch in the numbers for the watercolorist's house, which I always imagine painted in faded pastels, the edges running over the lines that define it. It rings twice, then the watercolorist picks up. It has happened before and I never know what to say to him.

"Hello? Hello?" His voice is tinged with sleepiness and panic.

"Do you have Prince Albert in a can?" I say to him. My hands shake.

"Oh, God, it's him again," he says, his words muffled, far off.

"Billy, damn it." Laney's voice, and his behind her, their words tumbling together in the sheets of his bed. "This stops, right now, tonight," she says, "Or from here on I only talk through the lawyer." She hesitates. I can see her, pulling the sheet up over her breasts, tucking her hair behind her ear. "Billy, please."

"I was missing you, wanted to see how things are."

"It's two in the morning. Things are dark and quiet." I hear him behind her saying *just hang up the phone.*

"Dad's here." I can hear him, too, as I say it, shutting down the computer, walking through the hall. The screen door bangs shut behind him.

"Yeah? How's the cancer coming along?" In her voice I hear her half smiling; for a long time Dad's illness was a joke between us, one of those little tent pegs that stake down the corner of a marriage.

"Well, not much change, but he's working on it."

She laughs a little, sighs.

"I'm gonna hang up now, Billy," she says. I say, "Yeah" and then she does. I hold the phone against my ear until it begins its machine-gun fire of beeps.

I figure to find Dad on the porch and follow him out with a couple of bourbons, to take in the night noises of tree peepers and distant highway traffic, but he isn't there. I look out into the fan of light from the house, at the glimmer of cans and bottles I have strewn there. Nothing but his Vette, shiny with dew in the driveway.

"Dad?" My voice sounds like any voice at night, like an intrusion, a rip in the surface of the quiet.

I set the bourbons on the porch rail and walk out in my shorts and bare feet, down the road a ways, until I find him next to the rise of fill dirt that surrounds the new self-storage facility being built, over by the runoff pond. He is doing the newspaper trick, folding the edges up into a lantern shape and twisting them closed. When I was a kid, he'd let the lanterns go on the Little League field behind us, would do it on Fourth of July instead of buying me bottle rockets or firecrackers. He'd argue that they were *better* than fireworks, but something about them those close summer nights struck me as off. They made no noise as they burned, and we watched them without a word. The whole endeavor was too . . . *ceremonial* somehow. I didn't have the words to say so then—I remember only standing beside him (my mother back at the house) and watching, but casting my attention toward the gut-shaking boom of the professional fireworks show at the football field, or the neighborhood rattle of firecracker strings, straining for the sound of them instead of all that quiet. Now, as then, he twists the ends closed and sets fire to them with his Zippo lighter. As heat fills the hollow paper it lifts into the air, slowly spinning.

"Dad?" He jumps, turns toward me just as the lantern tilts away from him and out over the pond.

"Billy, holy bejesus, what are you doing here?" The lantern tips and lands in the pond, burns a few seconds, then sinks.

"I just talked to Laney. The watercolorist was giving her stage directions the whole time."

He nods, opens and closes his lighter. "That's a shame. Shame you can't just let it alone, either."

"Well. And you, what the hell are you doing out here?"

"Oh, just that old paper trick I used to do. You know the one."

"Dad . . . that's not the question exactly. It's almost three o'clock in the morning."

He shrugs, snaps the lighter closed. "Couldn't sleep."

"So you walk into the woods to do some stunt from twenty-five years ago." I shake my head, noticing how cold I am. "You know, you might have a stronger case for Alzheimer's than cancer."

He laughs, pulls a cigar from his pocket, and busies himself unwrapping it. Even in the pale arc-lamp light from the construction site, I can see his face flushing.

"I just thought . . . we don't have a hell of a lot to reminisce over. I thought this might fit the bill. Every Independence Day, we did these, remember?"

"You're reminiscing by yourself?"

He chews his cigar. "I'm practicing."

I laugh. "Dad, we don't have to reminisce. We can just visit and talk. That fits the bill fine."

He looks suddenly old, standing there in his boxers and satin jacket. He has a stack of newspaper at his feet, two of them half-folded into lanterns.

"Well, listen," I tell him. "You went to all the trouble. Go ahead and do another one."

He shrugs. "Not like you're some little kid anymore," he says. "It would just be silly."

"We're out here at the self-storage site in our underwear, Dad. I think we're a little past silly."

He shrugs again, twists up one of the papers, and lights it. We stand back to watch the pale orange shadows of flame like something alive inside the folds of paper, the tiny curls of smoke, and then the turning and slow lift as heat fills the lantern. It was always like a contest, to see if it could get airborne before it consumed itself. The night breeze catches this one and pushes it up and out across the pond, where it settles atop the Porta Potti, and something—chemical fumes, methane gas—draws the flame in a blunt *whoosh* that bursts down the roof vent and into the toilet area, the white fiberglass walls suddenly in X-ray, showing through veiny brown, like a giant paper bag luminary at Christmas. The explosion is small, relatively, and self-extinguishing—it kicks open the door, then is quiet, the vent pipe trailing smoke.

The remaining papers at our feet scatter with the breeze out into the pond. We look at each other, the only sound a dog barking, far off.

"Okay," I say, "I guess I'm ready to sleep now." I grin at him, my old man of a father.

He grins back. "Conquering the world, one tiny shit house at a time."

. . .

By dawn, as on most any day of my growing up, Dad is off somewhere in the Vette, his cereal bowl and coffee cup left behind clean in the drainboard. I eat my cereal and punch the button to listen to Laney's voice. Instead I hear Dad's voice, overloud, the speaker crackling as he talks.

"HE, BILLY KESLER, ISN'T HERE AT HOME RIGHT NOW, SO THIS IS HIS MACHINE. YOU CAN LEAVE A MESSAGE FOR HIM IF YOU LIKE . . ." A few seconds of silence, then, "BILLY, I UPDATED THIS TAPE FOR YOU . . . HOPE YOU DON'T MIND. IF YOU DO, CHANGE IT BACK." I rewind all the way to the start, trying to find Laney's voice, but it isn't there to be found.

I drive to the community college campus, where I share an office with a professor of heating and air-conditioning. I go to class, hand back a batch of papers two weeks late. I show a short movie of *The Lottery* and we talk about religion and I assign a paper I will collect sometime near the day I return the current ones. This one kid, Kenny Pecora, follows me back to my office, wanting to know what else he can do. He has been to the Writing Center every day, he tells me. This is his third C in a row, he could lose his scholarship. He blinks at me, his face pale and desperate. When he opens his mouth, his teeth are overly large and square, like Teddy Roosevelt in the old photographs, smiling behind his pince-nez.

"I'm not mad at you, Mr. Kesler," he says. His hair is cut so short I can see his scalp beneath it. He is wearing a Led Zeppelin T-shirt and for half a weird minute I am twenty years old again, a sophomore wearing the same shirt, standing in line for a midnight show of *The Song Remains the Same.* "I'm just really, really frustrated, you know?" he says, and I have a near impulse to say, "Let me tell you about frustration," like I'm some cantankerous stereotype, a sour old man in a comic strip. But the truth is I'm a young man still, and most of what needs to be said to students never gets said. I never tell the ones I know won't make it. Never tell the A students they are wasting their time in a place like this, never say that half of teaching is being skilled at bullshit, that problems with comma splices and topic sentences will not destroy their lives. Right now I could tell Kenny Pecora that one day I will see his name in an old grade book when I'm cleaning out files and I will remember his Teddy Roosevelt teeth and think, *Oh, yeah . . . him,* and wonder for about six seconds what became of him, but not care too much because nothing much *will* come of him, good or bad. I could tell him that he may have a wife who thinks he's distant and takes off on him, and he may put his fist through the glass door of a toaster oven, or he may have a father who spends his retirement staging his own slow death, or he may frustrate a student with three Cs in a row because he has given up actually reading the papers. I could, but to what end? I used to be a good teacher and might be again, if I decided. Think of some high school jock, now old and fat and wearing out his ass on the couch, knowing he could, anytime he felt like it, get himself back into shape. Back into fighting weight. Hustle a mile or two around the block. Do a few bench presses. Get back into trim and the old corduroys. Maybe tomorrow, maybe the day after.

I tell Kenny Pecora to hang in there.

· · ·

After class Dad swings by to pick me up in his Vette, and we head out to the Noah's Ark construction site. He lets me drive, and I have to slide the seat way back from where he had it, noticing as I do how much thinner he's become. For a second I consider the possibility that he really *does* have cancer, but even God doesn't possess that much irony. Only enough to let someone's wife move in with the instructor of the class she was taking because the marriage counselor advised her to find some interests that belong only to her. That she did.

The ark is at the end of Cherry Hill Road, a project the local Baptist church is paying for with raffles and bake sales and the usual guilt. At the edge of town is a big, hand-painted wooden sign: WE ARE REBUILDING NOAH'S ARK! This is true, in a way, though I have trouble picturing Noah and his sons with a crane and steel girders and warning signs from OSHA, which this place has in abundance. As we pull up, we see a pair of workers in hard hats, sitting on the top girder eating lunch, like those old photos of New York City. Several other men lean on the hood of a truck, looking at blueprints.

"There it is," I say.

Dad half stands, so his head pops out of the open top of the car. "I'll be damned," he says down to me. "You can just see what it'll be like finished. Imagine old Noah fitting two of every animal inside there."

For a minute I give in to the story, trying to imagine it the way it was always shown in all those dentists' waiting room kids' Bible books. The ark is surprisingly compact, only about the size of a small office building, like it's meant not to hold animals but maybe just a dermatologist and an accountant or two. When it's finished, the paper said, they will hold Sunday school classes inside, with enough room left in the hull for a volleyball court.

My father keeps looking, muttering to himself. "Took him a hundred and twenty years to do it, and his neighbors all scoffed. 'Old Noah, the flake,' they'd say, 'Noah the nutcase.' But the man had him a vision, yessir. That he did."

I say nothing, wondering where all of this is coming from. The closest he has ever come to any kind of religion was forming the Tommy Kesler Society. All the time of my growing up, Sunday mornings for him meant three of his friends over for Bloody Marys and fishing shows on TV, while I slept in late hearing the mixed sounds of their hoots and whistles when the show's host landed a big one, and my mother beating eggs and frying bacon in the kitchen. When commercials came on, they would click over to the television preachers and spend those three minutes making fun of their haircuts and neckties and weeping, before fishing came on again.

My father shouts to the men looking at the blueprints. "Mind if we go up there? For maybe five minutes?"

They look at each other. "Who the hell are you?" one of them says.

"I'm Tommy Kesler."

The three of them stare, waiting for further explanation. When none is forthcoming, one of them shrugs and points to the signs posted on the side of the little trailer, with AUTHORIZED PERSONNEL ONLY written in big, red letters.

My father slumps back down in the seat. "You know, your mother would have liked this. She was always a big Noah fan."

"She was? Mom?" This seems weirder than his own sudden interest in Bible stories. I can recall not one conversation about religion around our house, except when the Baptist church sent out one of their SWAT teams, who sat my mother down in the living room (Dad was off selling pools), handed her tracts and opened their Bibles, bludgeoned her with hell and eternity and my own little eight-year-old unsaved soul, hitting her over the head with it. When they left, she slammed the door, tossed the tracts down the coal furnace vent, and told me the only problem with full-immersion baptism was that they bothered to yank them back up.

"Well, I'm guessing she was," Dad says. "Who wouldn't be?" The men high up finish lunch and begin working again, pounding thick hammers on the corners of the girders.

My department chair leaves a note in my box saying he'd like a word with me, which means students have been complaining. Twice now, Kenny Pecora has not shown up for class. For once, I wish he had, because I spent the hour reading and talking about an Elizabeth Bishop poem, the one about the armadillo and the fire balloons in Brazil, which my father put into my head by torching the Porta Potti. For the first time in a good while, I actually paid attention to what I was saying.

At home, as I pull up behind the Vette and get out of my car, I find a woman sitting on the front porch. She calls out "hello" and waves to me.

"Can I help you?" I say.

"No, I'm fine," she says. I stand below her on the bottom porch step, looking up at where she sits in the glider. She is a handful of years older than me, a plump, round-faced woman, though pretty and dark haired. She is working a crossword puzzle in *TV Guide,* filling it in with a golf pencil.

"I'm sorry," I say. "Who are you again?"

"Tommy didn't tell you?" she says. "I'm Wendy, the home health care nurse."

"No," I say. "Tommy didn't." I stand gawking at her, feeling stomach-punched. *What if?* I think. But no, he has pulled similar stuff before. The first month after he invented his cancer, he shaved off his eyebrows and rented a wheeled oxygen tank from a medical supply house.

"Where is he, anyway?" I ask her.

"I think taking a shower. He's really a sick man, you know."

My heart wobbles. "Why do you say that? I mean, what's your assessment?"

She shrugs. "Well, he said he is. Who would lie about that?" She lifts a bottle from beside the rocker and takes a dainty sip of St. Pauli Girl. I take a good long look at Wendy the home health care nurse, wondering where in hell he has found her. She smiles and asks me if I know the name of Red Skelton's lovable yokel, Clem something.

I find Dad in the kitchen, his hair wet from the shower, cooking eggs and hash browns.

"A home nurse?" I say to him.

"You know, she has never been out to see the ark, either. It's like New Yorkers, they live there forty years and never see the Statue of Liberty."

"Dad . . ."

"Toast or English muffin? Wendy took me to the store. Well, I took her, but same thing. You got another letter from the lawyers."

I shrug. "Why do you think you need a nurse? And what kind of nurse drinks beer at three o'clock in the afternoon?"

"I asked her to drink beer with me. Part of her job. That and

watch some TV, a few hands of hearts, a shoulder rub or two."
He folds the omelet, then flips it in the air.

"She isn't a nurse, is she, Dad?"

"If you mean the *Good Housekeeping* seal of some university big-shot degree, then no. But 'nurse' is just a *function*, Billy. A plumber could be a nurse, a cowboy or a baker could, too."

"Or a contractual college instructor," I say. I see what he's up to: he wants to shame me into letting him stay on, into midnight reminiscences, into feeling sorry for him in his relatively old age by hiring someone when I fail to do it.

"Hey, who's making dinner here? Who cleaned the house today, you or me?"

"So where did you hire your nurse? From the local bakery or the local cattle drive?"

He flips his omelet, twice this time, catches it, slides it out onto a plate. "She works for an escort service. But it is just escort, Billy, no hanky-panky."

I shake my head and half laugh. "Dad, this whole thing is hanky-panky." I help him butter the toast.

He looks around the kitchen. "What whole thing?"

"Your reason for coming here, your cancer. All just more of your stunts. Problem is, I'm not really entertained by it anymore."

"So I come here to make amends, and this is how I'm treated."

"I don't want you to make any amends," I tell him, and it's true. What's the point? Everyone has amends to make, so no one does. They all cancel each other out.

Just then Wendy walks in and opens the refrigerator for another beer. "Kadiddlehopper," she says.

I look at her. "Pardon?"

"That was the answer. On the crossword." She is a little bit drunk. Dad finishes fixing the plates and we sit on the counter barstools to eat. We don't say much. Wendy continues writing in the answers to her puzzle. Finally Dad interrupts the scrape and ring of silverware.

"Wendy, tell Doubting Billy here your opinion of my condition."

"Dad . . ."

"Well," she wipes her mouth, slips the pencil behind her ear. "Your Dad is not well, Billy."

"Is that an official diagnosis, or did you find that in *TV Guide?*"

She laughs, her face flushing deep red, then retrieves her pencil.

Dad sets down his fork, folds his hands. "You want to call my doctor, smart guy? I'll give you the number."

I look at the shadow of dark ringing his head as his hair grows in, sunburn peeling the tops of his ears, the hard set of his mouth. "Yeah, I would like to do that. Give me the number. Does he have a name, or do you need to think about it some?"

He borrows Wendy's pencil and writes a number down on his napkin, still looking at me. "Dr. Snelson," he says. "You'll be sorry."

Wendy holds up her hand for us to be quiet. " 'Early-TV pie guy, Soupy *blank*,' " she says, reading from her puzzle. "Does anyone know?"

An hour later I'm sitting on the bed with the cordless phone in one hand and the napkin in the other. Dad and Wendy are talking in the living room, where I left them watching some movie of the week, sitting on the couch drinking beer and holding hands like teenagers. I punch the numbers for Dr. Snelson and get his machine, a woman's voice reminding me of regular office hours, telling me to go to the hospital if I need immediate attention, or to call the doctor's pager if this is an emergency. I write down his beeper number, wondering briefly what the difference is between an emergency and needing immediate attention.

Sitting there on my marriage bed, I start to punch in the beeper number but with one tiny swerve, a little joggle in my brain, instead allow my fingers to punch in the number for the watercolorist's house. Laney picks up on the second ring.

"I think my father has cancer," I tell her.

"Very funny, Billy. I said not to call, okay? I mean it. I'm trying to be decent about this."

"No, really. I think he really does have cancer."

She is silent a moment.

"So you've talked to his doctor then, right?"

I look down at the folded napkin. "Not exactly."

"What then?"

I stop for a minute, trying to think what evidence I actually do have. "I had to move back the seat on the Vette when I drove it. Way back."

"Dammit, Billy—"

"And he hired a home nurse. Sort of."

I hear her draw in her breath and let it out, and I can see from the sound of it the way it puffs her bangs up and away from her eyes. "You are two of a kind, you know that? And this is a new low, Billy. It really is."

"Laney—"

"Listen, I didn't want to go along with this, but Dennis installed caller ID for me and from now on if it's you, I'm not going to pick up, Billy, okay? You understand me?"

"Who's Dennis?" I say. This is enough to make her hang up, which she does with the softest click of the phone.

In the living room Wendy the home nurse is asleep on the couch with her head tipped back and mouth open, the TV muted, my father just sitting and looking at the faces on the screen.

"I need to drive her home," he stage-whispers to me.

"Let her stay," I say aloud. "She's out anyway. Toss a blanket over her, and we'll fix her pancakes in the morning."

"Good enough." He nods and we look at each other, then the TV, the faces moving their mouths.

"You can take me out, though," I finally say.

"Kinda late for a drive."

"I want to see them," I say. "Together in that house. I want to look in the living room window and see them sitting on the couch, like you two, holding hands." I rub my mouth with my fingers. "I think I need to see that."

He clicks off the TV and Wendy stirs a little, mutters in her sleep. "I think you like the idea of seeing that," he says. "Two hours afterward, you'll feel like an idiot."

"I can go by myself," I say.

Ten minutes later we're in the Corvette moving through the night toward a subdivision named Rolling Hills. Dad is driving, smoking another of the cigars he had all but given up since he pretended to have cancer. When we finally find the right address, the house is dark and still. On the side porch is one of those ultraviolet bug-zapping lights. We sit in the dark with the engine idling, the house quiet and sleeping, the bug light giving off an electric buzz every few seconds. The watercolorist has a mailbox shaped like a red barn, a canoe strapped to his Volvo. A patch of dandelions grows beneath his drier vent. There is nothing to see.

"You're right," I say. "Not even two hours, and I feel like an idiot."

"Not much to it, is there?" He pats my knee. "There never is." I shake my head. "Let's go home."

We take off down the quiet streets, and Dad reaches under the seat between his legs and then plugs in a cassette tape of Irish music, filling the close car with flutes and guitar. As he taps his fingers on the dash, it occurs to me that what I know of him is just some little edge of who he actually is, a tiny percentage of him. In all the photos I have from childhood, my father is always a blur, jumping into the frame at the last second, or out of it, the top of his head or side of his face cut off. He is like that still, always.

"What I want to know," he says suddenly, "is why you two never had a kid. That might've been the glue you needed."

"I wanted to wait until I got away from the community college, landed a real teaching job." I shrug. "In its own clock-punching, dental-plan way, it *is* real, I guess. And I wish we had now, so there'd be some connection. This way, everything is so damn *clean*. She packs, and she's gone."

He nods but doesn't answer. I notice that while I've been talking he's gone past the Braddock Road exit and is heading toward Cherry Hill Road, toward the ark.

"All right, what's with you and all this Noah stuff?" I say. "Have you gone religious on me?"

He waves the back of his hand, then looks at his cigar and

tosses it out the window. "Nah, nothing like that, son. I just like the way the story's lasted so long. I mean, it's how old? God knows. One website pegged the thing on the Babylonians and those other guys, the Sumerians, and here we are in the space age, telling it all over again with steel and cement."

I don't bother pointing out to him that we are about thirty years past the space age. "The eternal verities," I say.

"And what's that, professor?"

"Faulkner, talking about eternal truths."

He frowns. "Hell, I don't give a tinker's damn about the truth. And I don't care if it's a story or a good lie or a fairy tale or what have you. The longevity of it—that's your meat and potatoes."

He looks over at me, to see if this has made an impression. "Besides," he says, "those bastards today wouldn't give us a fair look."

"And?"

"I want to see it. Up close."

"It's trespassing, Dad. We could get in real trouble."

"Doctors gave up on the radiation treatments two months ago. I'm supposed to care about trouble?"

I shake my head, look out the window into the dark. "Dad . . ."

"Did you make that phone call, Billy? To Snelson?"

"Nope."

"You going to?" I see him looking at me, cutting his eyes.

I think about this while he slides up to the top of the exit and does not even slow down for the stop sign, swinging out onto the narrow road. The napkin with Dr. Snelson's beeper number is still folded away inside my pocket. I wonder if anybody ever *once* called my father's bluff, over anything. But no matter what news I get from the doctor, dialing that number will mean either that I don't believe my father's truth or I don't buy into his bullshit. I don't know which would wound him deeper. "I'm not sure," I tell him. He starts to say something else, then changes his mind.

The reds and browns of the structural steel are all rendered black against the deep blue of the night sky. We get out and walk toward the ark, the only light a yellow bulb, no brighter than a nightlight, on the side of the construction trailer. The path turns from gravel to mud, my shoes sinking in. Down across the hill from us, sparse traffic slips along the highway, the truckers gearing down for the long climb into the mountain.

Dad braces his foot against the bottom scaffolding and begins hauling himself up in slow steps. "You know the part that gets me?" he says, looking down at me. "He was in the damn desert."

I start my own climb, the rust on the iron bars scaling my palms. "I think the part that gets you is that nobody believed him, and he was right, and everyone that doubted him met a horrible death."

He laughs. "Yeah, that, too."

By now he is puffing hard, his legs above me quivering. We walk out and sit on one of the girders, not at the top, but high enough to make me nervous. Off in the distance I can see the lights of the next town, a faint glow rising up. We sit side-by-side, dangling our legs over, like the men earlier with their lunch pails. When the wind blows, even lightly, the whole structure shakes a little.

"I know what you'd like," my father says.

"What's that?"

"If it started raining right now."

I laugh out loud. "True, I'm a sucker for easy irony."

"You know Noah put the bigger animals—your elephants, your camels, what have you—on the lower levels. That way he eliminated the need for ballast. Pretty damn brainy."

"Uh-huh. Where are you getting this stuff?"

"Told you, from websites. All these nuts still looking for 'the real Noah's Ark.' One of them's an astronaut. They're missing the point." He raises the collar of his Corvette jacket, shivering a little.

"Which is?"

"Validation. We all want stories told about us a long time after we're gone. We all want to be Noah, or his ark."

"True ones or lies . . . doesn't matter, huh?"

He taps my thigh with his fist. "You got it, bub."

"Speaking of stories, why don't you tell me once and for all about the cancer?"

"I had my say, junior." He takes another cigar and the Zippo from his pocket, unwraps the cellophane, and lets it fall away. "You've still got that number, don't you? Or did you lose it already?"

I pull the napkin from my jeans and unfold it. He frowns, nods.

"And how about *you*, once and for all?" he says. "You plan to keep phoning that girl? My vote is cease and desist."

The night is cloudless, faint stars visible above the lights from the surrounding towns. Laney used to take us far away from the lights, out into the country near Pigeon Creek, down washed-out dirt roads where we could watch the smear of stars away from the lights of town, where I would ask her to name them for me, over and over. I would tell her that those nights were the reason she majored in astronomy. By now, I imagine, she has pasted stars to the watercolorist's ceiling and has named the constellations for him, charming him with reruns.

"That's pretty much done with," I say. "But I do have another call to make."

He glances down at the paper, jams the cigar in his mouth, lights it. "You know, Billy, I'm thinking I ought to head out tomorrow," he says. "Drop Wendy off where I found her, then find my way north."

"I have to call Kenny Pecora." I take his lighter from him, the chrome case still warm, and flick it, the flame swirling blue and yellow. My father's face draws down with confusion.

"Who the hell is Kenny Pecora?" he asks, still eyeing the napkin.

"Student of mine," I say. "He looks like Teddy Roosevelt." My father watches me as he puffs his cigar.

We sit, quiet, gripping the steel girders in a cloud of early autumn chill and cigar smoke, the lighter burning my fingers, our legs touching, dangling. It is this image of us I will recall seven months later, in the minutes after the phone finally rings on my desk at work and it is Dr. Snelson calling me, his words circling back like the answer to a question sent out that night: how I held the edge of the napkin in the flame, how the igniting brightened our faces, how I let it go and we watched as the paper fell, carried on faint breezes, burning down and down into the dark water that surrounds us all.

The Properties of Stainless Steel

A single tree dominates our backyard, a tall white oak full of squirrel nests, the top flashing a Mylar balloon that settled in a few years ago. It's one of those twin trees, the base split into two trunks grown up in a big V shape. I used to imagine making a slingshot of it, between the trunks, halfway up, taking aim on Winston-Salem and pelting them with baseballs, apples, cans of tuna fish. This big, unsolved mystery, the sky raining garbage, and me lurking at the bottom of it all. But those ideas wither away after Rhonda begins her habit of gazing out the kitchen screen door while she chain-smokes, pondering that tree and its separate trunks. I know what she's up to in her mind. We used to talk about fitting a treehouse between those split trunks, how I would nail it up for a birthday surprise. Now I think Rhonda just sees the tree as us, sees it as everything that our first counseling session taught us was wrong with our marriage. I've thought of pointing out that the tree at its root is still connected, despite the split, but she would have no interest in hearing me try to explain her private notions.

Before we left Family Services that first Wednesday, our counselor, Dr. Goodwin, told Rhonda and me that our "homework" was to find a common interest. Dr. Goodwin looked at us with her sad, practiced smile, the table beside our couch stacked with Kleenex dispensers and board games designed to coax different groups into talking about their troubles. One of the games, its cardboard box torn and faded, was called *1 . . . 2 . . . 3 . . . 12 Step!* Another was *Count on Me!* I was thinking they were probably the kinds of games where everyone wins, and wondering just what the hell that's supposed to teach anybody, when Dr. Goodwin interrupted my thoughts. She told Rhonda and me that we should search for ways to spend unstructured time together. Finding something you both like, she said, will keep you from healing in different directions. I nodded and said nothing, thinking that was our problem already: too much in common, nearly all of it sadness. Rhonda started the silent crying she did so easily after the months of practice, tears marking her face but not a sound from her. The way an actress cries on the screen, I thought. Only this was no acting. It was the baby we didn't have anymore. Or it was me, never sad enough or the right way to suit her. She turned away. We sat, the three of us, trapped in our silences, in the fourth silence which had brought us all together here. We said nothing, as if waiting for the skies to begin their mysterious rain.

.   .   .

The next morning Rhonda found—in the newspaper, the way you'd find a missing dog—our common interest.

"Folk dancing," she said. She laid the paper on the kitchen table and tapped it with her finger. "The Lower Cape Fear Dance Society presents. Live band, wooden floor . . . this is the one, Curt."

"What one?"

"Our together thing. Folk dancing."

"So we save our marriage by dancing to fiddle music." I half laughed. "Think Dr. Goodwin will write us a prescription?"

She watched me with those tired eyes. "It's not a joke, Curt. We mess up this marriage, it can't be repaired. We're all we have anymore."

I nodded, reminding myself how well I knew this woman, how I could recognize the sound of her footsteps in a crowded mall. "So we just find a common interest at random." I shrugged. "Just open the paper and grab one."

"Planning has gotten us here," she said. "I'm willing to try a blind stab or two."

The dance is Saturday night in an old building next to the junior high where they used to store lawn mowers. The inside has a dusty wooden floor, ceiling fans, and a string band of two men with beards and a woman wearing a top hat. We've come early, for the five-dollar lessons. Our instructor is this little troll of a guy named Phil, with rainbow suspenders holding up his hiking shorts. He wears muddy boots and a ponytail; he has bad skin. I know I would not even hire this guy for my cleaning crew, but I don't say anything. This is Rhonda's night, and I intend to go along.

Phil shows us all the moves we have to know before the caller starts the first dance. We learn do-si-do and allemande and promenade. We learn cast-off and handy-hand. We stay in motion, and I start to like it okay. The people there are not what I expected, not the Roy Rogers and Dale Evans types in neckerchiefs and puffy skirts, but all these aging hippies like you see at the Arts Fest in the park downtown, braless women with big silver earrings, and men with sideburns and Jesus sandals. I feel out of place in my striped golf shirt and blue jeans, which Rhonda ironed for me with a crease down the front. But she thinks I look handsome and that's good enough.

She squeezes my hand while we try the most basic step, balance and swing. We spin each other into dizziness while Phil keeps shouting for everyone to *use* that centrifugal force, to *lean* back into each other's grip.

"Give weight!" he says. "Give weight, give weight!" He keeps hovering over us, touching our shoulders and arms. My back is sweaty, and Phil is getting on my nerves. My feet feel clumsy, dumb.

"Please try to like this," Rhonda says, anxious about me.

"I like it fine," I say, and she smiles at me, squeezes my hand again.

"No, no, no, no, NO!" Phil runs up behind me. His name tag slips from suspenders and flutters to the floor. "Not ring-around-the-rosie," he says to me. Everybody laughs and I feel my ears warm. "Give your weight, and keep your inside foot *planted*, like a pivot in basketball."

"You want to go a little one-on-one?" I say. It's my turn to get a laugh, though I hadn't meant to. Rhonda laughs, too, and this feels good to me, this getting along. It has been a while, and the arguments have gotten progressively stupid, the last one because I'd thrown a July Fourth barbeque for my work crew and their girlfriends, and late that night we'd poured vodka into the dog's dish (Bixby, Rhonda's husky), then laughed as he teetered around and walked into the kitchen cabinets. Rhonda did not find this funny in the least, and neither did I the next morning when the memory of it sank through layers of my wounded skull, but it was too late for apology. The general theme of all our arguments has been my lack of sympathy, not just for her but for us, for myself. When the baby died early last year, I went looking for reasons: Rhonda kept smoking the first month; she hadn't always taken her vitamins; I hadn't watched over her enough; my small floor cleaning business didn't take in enough to let her quit her job. Any of these seemed likely, but they seemed to Rhonda only like blame. What I still want somebody to explain to me is the difference between cause and blame—where do those two part company?

Soon enough I get the hang of balance and swing, and when the music kicks in for our first practice dance, I fall right in. Dance feels good in my bones, like work except you'd never have cause to curse it. I'm glad enough not to be at work, to let my crew polish the floors themselves for one night. We get locked in every night at Kmart to sweep and wax the floors, vacuum the carpeted areas. Once the manager throws home the front bolt, there is no way out of the building. My crew finishes the job quickly, working like sled dogs, so as to have the bulk of the night off to raid the snack bar, turn on the TVs in the appliance department, crank up the stereos, ride bicycles through the aisles.

I stand off to one side while Phil borrows Rhonda to demonstrate for everybody the right way to execute a California twirl.

He spins her fast so her blue cotton skirt swirls out and up past her knees, giving us all a glimpse of her pretty legs, sturdy in their low heels, and when she stops, the skirt swirls and wraps up around her thighs, then settles back. This is a thing I like to see, this glimpse of my wife's legs as if they are someone else's. When the demo ends, everyone claps. She pushes a strand of hair off her forehead and blushes with the heat and attention, smiling.

"All right, now. We're doing great, folks," Phil says, drunk on his own false cheer. I feel like reminding him he's getting paid for this, that "folks" is not a word anybody uses anymore.

While the band retunes, we get ourselves paper cups of water out of the cooler. People file in the door, pulling the cold in behind them, shuffing off their coats, blowing into their hands. I imagine this place from the outside, how inviting it must look: a tiny building set off in the cold, giving off its light and heat and music. When we arrived, I hadn't noticed this.

The band members introduce themselves while the folding chairs along the walls fill up with people, many of them old ladies dressed up in dangling earrings and carrying beaded purses, wearing smudges of rouge, like this is their big night on the town.

"I feel sorry for them," Rhonda says after I point them out to her. "Hoping to meet Mr. Right." She smiles a little.

"At this point, most of their Mr. Rights are probably dead and buried."

Rhonda's smile vanishes. "You are just so cold sometimes, Curt," she says. "Those women are lonely."

But I know it is not my joke as much as it is my mention of the word: *death*. It is something we are supposed to have silently agreed to banish from our vocabularies, ignoring the black gash it has torn through our lives. Sometimes it's like a meteor has ripped through our house, left huge holes in the roof and floor, and we step around them, ignoring the rain that pours in, the cold, the weeds growing into our living room. Just keep stepping around.

We dance through the evening, the smell of perfumed sweat filling the little building, the windows steaming over. The old ladies occupying the folding chairs in their wilting dresses try to keep their gazes interested and curious, expectant. Like any moment, some good thing might happen. A couple times, I ask them to dance. I smile like a salesman and dance gently; they smell of powder and ammonia. The bones of their hands and ribs feel as fragile as bird bones. I almost envy them, for how imminent their deaths are, how perfectly placed at the end of their long years. Just where it is supposed to be. All my life death has been cutting ahead in line: first my father, a heart attack at forty-two, my mother of ovarian cancer at fifty-six, and now my daughter, at eleven months, killed by a fucking acronym. When we finish dancing, they kiss my cheek or squeeze my hand. Rhonda tells me I'm a sweetheart.

Friday night at Kmart, after the floors are all done, the boys throw a party. I allow this for certain occasions, and lately I've allowed it more and more. Party the rest of your lives, I feel like telling them. Tonight is Corliss's birthday, plus Danny and Lisa's first wedding anniversary. They all bring along wives and girlfriends. The assistant manager gives me a look before he locks me in, but he doesn't say anything; as long as the place is shiny clean at 8:00 A.M. he doesn't really care what happens while it's dark.

The boys work fast and by one o'clock the place is scrubbed

and the supplies are back in the storeroom. Danny cranks up all
the stereos in the appliance department to the same station, and
while Led Zeppelin rattles the counters, we dig bags of stale popcorn out of the snack bar. On the returns shelf in the back they
find open packages of candy bars and Red Hots. The boys have all
brought small coolers loaded with six-packs. Lisa and Danny start
dancing in the aisle beside sporting goods, where a large empty
space waits to be made into the garden center for spring. Lisa is
eight months pregnant, and I stand watching her, the high, clear
glow of her skin, the sway of her back. I keep bugging her to quit
smoking. I remember how relieved we were after the first
trimester with all its sickness and worry, how Rhonda invented
cravings she did not really have just so she could send me out in
the middle of the night for bean burritos or Milky Ways. This
was my part of her pregnancy, helping her learn to breathe,
feeding her, all the usual. We gave into it, feeling corny. A kid
feeling, like playing house, like you could take a good thing and
make it last forever. We believed that for a while. Stupid.

Carlo and his girlfriend Tammy borrow a couple of bikes from
sporting goods and ride in circles around the store, disappearing for minutes at a time, their whoops and laughs echoing
around us. The rest of us sit in the snack bar drinking beer,
watching the dancers, waiting for the bicyclers to show up again.
Wilson shows us where the doctors put the pins in his arm after
his motocross accident. From that we are drawn into the usual
drinking habit of trading stories and scars. I show them mine
from when the lawnmower sent a roofing nail into my leg.

"That hardly even counts, Curt," Terry says, and pulls up his
shirt to show us a foot-long scar across his chest from a car
wreck when he was sixteen.

"My Uncle Don has a bullet in his jaw from Vietnam," Wilson says. "You can see this little lump."

"My roommate has a polycarbon rod in his arm," Terry says. "Broke it operating a jackhammer."

"I went to grade school with this kid, had a metal plate in his head," I tell them. "You could see the dent in his skull." They all laugh at this, the girls making faces.

"No way," Terry says. "What was his name?"

I shake my head. "I don't remember. Too long ago."

This is a lie, but I don't feel like talking about him. It *is* too long, and it's not a funny story. Joseph Turlow had been in my class since third grade, and he did have a metal plate in his head following surgery to correct a benign tumor putting pressure on his brain. But we didn't learn anything about the plate or the tumor until the sixth grade, when Mr. Levine was our teacher. Until then, everyone had pretty much ignored Joseph, afraid of his injury, of our imaginings about that metal plate. He was a fat kid, with a constant dewy sprinkling of sweat on the skin under his eyes. His teeth protruded at odd angles. His ears were overly small. All of this—what we might otherwise have thought of as the normal, awkward differences we all had (in my case, freckles and ears that stuck out)—instead seemed connected to the metal plate, as if his ugliness had been created in him or attached to him, much like the plate itself. We stayed away, averted our eyes, stole looks at the dent on his head, the clipped hair there that seemed to grow in a different direction from the rest. He sat at the end of our lunchroom table, and at recess spent his half hour hurling rocks over the fence. I felt bad for him, as I suspect everyone did, but our whispered knowledge of the plate in his head formed a barrier through which we were not able to approach him.

All of this Mr. Levine attempted to change. He told us one day that we all might learn from Joseph, then called him up to the front of the class and made him explain about the operation. Joseph stared at the pair of flags in their brass stands while he mumbled the details, his face darkening as he spoke, sweat dripping from the tip of his nose. Everyone looked away, some trying not to laugh. Mr. Levine sat on the edge of his desk with his legs crossed, watching Joseph and thoughtfully stroking his chin. Joseph knew all the words associated with his illness, and spoke about his dura and brain stem, about the tools they had used on him. He said these words the way a parrot might, with no apparent understanding of them. When he finished, Mr. Levine asked if we had any questions, then produced and passed around a plate of iron he said was the approximate size and shape of Joseph's. From this he segued into a discussion of magnetics and the properties of stainless steel. Joseph seemed unaffected by this, though after we left in the spring for Easter vacation he never came back. I didn't understand why I felt so bad for him. What I wanted all those years, I thought, was for people to stop ignoring Joseph for his steel plate, to accept it the way we accepted and joked about our own crossed eyes or glasses or out-of-style clothes. But when Mr. Levine had tried to do just that, it seemed like the worst thing I'd ever watched. I thought then, and think now, that the worst of our anguish we carry in our bowels, part of the rhythm of daily life, but hidden, not discussed or shown— not to our classmates, our science teachers, our husbands or wives.

. . .

Saturday night we went back to the dance. Things that week had seemed better, and on Wednesday I did not fight with Dr. Goodwin. We were able to go shopping together again at Food-4-Less, as we had always done before, making a game of our chores, but had not done since Sarah died. The shopping cart with the bolted-on baby seat was now just another useless device. Rhonda pushed past it without looking, but once we were inside, I fell back into old jokes—sneaking grapes out of the bag, sacking up and weighing one peanut—and soon had her smiling. These were old roles we were playing; the memorized lines came easily.

We are late this time and miss most of the lessons. Phil is finishing up, wiping his face with a bandanna while the band retunes. We start to practice our balance and swing.

"No, no, Rhonda," I say. "Both at the same time: balance *and* swing, not balance *or* swing." She laughs out loud.

"Let's make a pact not to step on each other," she says.

I shake her hand. "Deal."

"Remember everything Phil taught us."

"Phil who?" She laughs again, and I pull close and kiss the side of her face.

There is a strong grip on my shoulder and I turn to face Robert Olander, who was manager of Kmart the year I started the cleaning contracting business. He'd been transferred only a month before Sarah died.

"Curt, good as hell to see you," he says, pumping my hand. His voice is low, and I can barely hear him over the noise of the band, of people talking and laughing. "This is Rhonda, then. Good to see you out."

I'm surprised to hear him call Rhonda by name, as they have

never met. But worse is his tone of conciliation, of pity. I feel my stomach clench up.

"I was sorry to hear of . . . about your losing the baby," he says. He looks at me. "Mr. Comensoli told me at a manager's meeting."

"Thank you for thinking of us," Rhonda says, practiced at saying the right things.

"Yes, Robert," I say, "but we didn't lose her." Rhonda squeezes my hand, her nails in my palm.

Robert snaps to attention. "I understood . . . I mean . . . I was given to believe—"

"She died," I say. "God, if only we had just *lost* her, right? Then we could go out and find her. We could put an ad in the paper."

"Curt," Rhonda says.

"Misplaced," I say. "There's a diagnosis I could live with."

"Curt, I understand this is difficult . . ." Robert says.

"It is, Robert," I say. "It's very difficult. I'm sorry. You should ignore me." My voice is shaking, and I jam my hands into my pockets. Rhonda is crying. Robert blushes, his eyes cutting around the room while he nods at me. I suddenly feel sorry for him, which feels a hell of a lot better than the other way around. This was something I wish I could have told Joseph Turlow: Feel sorry for *us,* Joe. Make *us* uncomfortable, make *us* question God because of your existence. Rub our faces in you.

"You're in our prayers, Curt," Robert says. He shrugs. I shake his hand and apologize again, let him make his escape from me.

"Let's go," I say to Rhonda.

For a few moments she doesn't say anything. She wipes her eyes, squares her chin. "You go if you want, I'm dancing."

I nod. "Okay. I'll wait." I sit for a while by the door, in one of the folding chairs that a little while later the old ladies in their dresses will fill. The dance lines begin to form as the caller steps up on a chair at the front of the room, a microphone in her hand. They begin a walk-through of the dance, and my eyes search out Rhonda, who is partnered with Phil, near the front of the line. I see him point to her feet, giving her further instruction in the fast twirling of the balance and swing, which still gives her problems. All week she has made us practice this basic step, in the kitchen while the pasta was boiling, in the den during commercials.

The caller makes jokes and everyone laughs. The windows are already covered with moisture; against one flutters a large white moth, tangled in spiderweb. The music kicks in and the dance begins in full, a couple dozen pairs of feet shuffling and stomping in unison. It's a good noise; I go outside to escape it.

Outside is frigid, a bright, icy moon in the trees. I sit on the cold steps and watch the cars zoom past on the road, some with headlights missing, some stereos thumping. From one car a cigarette gets tossed, and it bounces behind in the dark, throwing up sparks like little fireworks. Dancers are still arriving, shrugging their shoulders against the cold as they move across the lot. A German shepherd barks at them from the bed of a red pickup truck. People nod hello as they arrive, step around me into the building. One man moves across the parking lot with an exaggerated limp while a younger couple, who seem to be with him, moves patiently behind him, holding hands. His progress is slow; though he is hard to make out in the dark, each step seems to involve a complex series of mechanized movements. Like the others, he nods hello as he makes his slow, incremental progress up the stairs. I smile at him, exaggerate my pretense of not noticing his difficulties, relieved when finally he makes it past me. It is quiet now outside; I sit there until my butt feels numb, my hands stiff.

Inside, Rhonda is flush-faced and damp, like all the other dancers. The heat hits me all at once, like stepping into a greenhouse. When they finish drinking their water, the dancers take the floor again, the caller shuffling her note cards. Rhonda smiles at the man beside her; he leans next to her, pointing at the band, making some small-talk joke. I sit next to one of the old ladies, who has come in without my noticing. When Rhonda starts for the floor with the man, I realize that he is the man from outside, with the limp. His left leg seems twisted beneath the long pants he wears, and the shoe on his left foot has a sole at least four inches thick. Even from where I sit I can hear the creak of braces on his legs, something I hadn't heard before, in the cold. With each step he has to lean far out to his left and bring his leg around in a circle, dragged by nothing more than his momentum. Again I think of Joseph Turlow, and it occurs to me that once you have decided to notice it, ruin is everywhere.

They make it okay through the walk-through, though the man (his nametag, I see as they move closer, reads "Tom") is sweating heavily. Unlike everyone else here, he wears long pants and long shirtsleeves, and his dancing must be twice the effort of anyone else's. They slowly walk through the balance and swing, Rhonda looking at her feet as she always does, uncertain, while Tom pivots easily on his big shoe. Then the walk-through is finished and they head back to their original places in the line, Tom dragging his foot and smiling, holding her hand.

Then the music starts up, full of banjo and fiddle. The caller sends out directions through the PA system, staying just ahead of the next move the dancers make. Tom and Rhonda work their way through the parts of the dance, walking down past the line around the outside, then back up through the middle, spinning into their allemandes and castoffs; it is all pretty easy after a while. While they move through the paces I silently count off the beats of the music, hoping they don't fall behind. Several times when they advance up or down the line, the next couple they are to dance with is already there, waiting for them to catch up. Tom is huffing now, smiling all the time with his big teeth, the back of his shirt damp. His limp becomes more pronounced—he is tiring, I guess—and he has to bob and weave his way through a single step. A couple times I find myself silently urging him, hurrying him along from within me, like when you're a passenger in someone's car, pressing an imaginary gas pedal. Rhonda seems not to notice, or else she covers well; I can't decide which. She smiles at him, laughs when they twirl. She must be the highlight of his night, I decide.

I'm glad that she found us the dancing. Rhonda was right, and so was Dr. Goodwin in her own abstract way. This has given us something else to look at together besides the scratches along the wall where the crib sat for nearly a year, besides the big Sears Christmas photo in the pewter frame on the bookshelf. We are learning these simple things together . . . steps, literally, like learning to walk all over again. One easy thing at a time.

Tom and Rhonda have advanced in the line and are now near me, standing under one of the ceiling fans. I give a little wave to Rhonda and smile, and she arches her eyebrows at me. Just then Tom grabs her up for a balance and swing, all those feet stomping in unison, and she looks back at me as Tom begins to pivot on his big shoe. She looks down at her own feet, still unsure, as Tom holds her waist and lifts her arm, and her pivot foot, as if trying to find its place by itself, slides fully in between Tom's legs. I watch this, and it seems like a magic trick waiting to happen, that in the next half second as his leg swings back around, it will meet her shin and somehow pass right through it, like a scarf through a ring. Instead their feet tangle, Rhonda cries out, and Tom pitches forward chest first onto the floor. He lands with all his weight on his chin and sternum, the sound like a bowling ball hitting the floor. Rhonda's hands fly up to her mouth and Tom's face freezes into its wide smile, and already he is protesting that he's fine, he's okay, while this chorus of noise rises up over the string sounds. Tom's feet drum against the wooden floor, trying to find traction, his hands trapped under him. The line stops, people bumping into one another, craning their necks to see the trouble. Rhonda looks over at me, and when she does I realize I'm doing nothing but sitting here, not jumping up to help. I shake my head and look at her, feeling once again the helplessness which seems to have taken root in me. I start to get up, then two of the men from the line are there picking Tom up by his arms, patting his back. He smiles, shaking his head, and I hear him say that he thought it was part of the dance. Everyone laughs big over this, let off the hook, relieved. Rhonda keeps dancing with him, but even from here I can see how shaken she is, her lips a thin white line.

When they finish I watch her smile as he thanks her, bowing to her a little. She rushes over to me, her eyes already starting to rim up.

"Let's please go," she says.

"It wasn't your fault," I tell her.

"No, it never is. Everything just crashes down all around me."

In the dark of the parking lot I hear the next song starting up, the sound of it muffled, made brittle by the cold.

. . .

The next few days we don't say much. There is no more talk of upcoming dances. Rhonda spends more time looking through the back window, past the tree with the split trunk, out into nothing. She doesn't even seem to see the tree anymore. She cancels our next appointment with Dr. Goodwin, and silence settles over our house the way it did just after Sarah died. Wednesday would have been her second birthday, so, as planned, we head out to Greenview to visit her gravesite. We have stopped bringing flowers, saying it is because they are always stolen. What we don't say is that it just seems so useless, the emptiest of gestures.

At Greenview, a fast-food paper cup sits on the ground beside Sarah's brass marker. Nearby are the leftovers from a campfire some kids have lit, sections of charred logs, blackened Coke cans and beer bottles. Down the hill below us, two boys are bundled up in denim jackets, fishing out of the small pond. We stand there a while, reading the words that seem so old by now.

"I don't know what to say anymore," Rhonda says.

I shrug. "I don't think there is anything. There is no *thing* to say."

She slips her fingers into mine. "It stops seeming real after a time, I think. I keep telling myself I shouldn't let that happen, let it become unreal. It's the easy way out."

"Well, but it's not real," I say. I kick over the cup, and the leavings of a milkshake pour out. "*That's* more real. A milkshake. You can understand a milkshake, get your brain around it."

She nods. "When that man fell, I thought for a moment I'd killed him."

"He fell because his legs are screwed up. They always have been, I bet. At least he knew what it meant when he fell, why it happens."

"You don't know that, Curt. He might cry every night of his life. He might put his fist through walls."

"He might. I'd even say he should. But it does no good, for him or us. There's no proper response. Hell, there is no response, proper or not. I don't have one, do you?"

She shakes her head.

"How about you?" I shout across the lawn. "You have one?" The kids look up from their fishing and then away from us. The wind picks up, our breath coming in white mists.

"Why don't you come with me to work tonight," I say. I take her hand.

"You never ask me."

"Well, I am now. It's a party. Come be with me."

She nods. "Okay."

We stand for a while longer before we go. I leave the milkshake cup where it is.

That night at Kmart, Rhonda right away starts in talking with Lisa, feeling her distended stomach, asking her about breastfeeding and epidurals. It's like she wants to meet this head on, these moments I only want to avoid. With everyone pitching in we finish the floors by midnight, and then the boys and their wives and girlfriends, so practiced by now, start the music and the beer and the snacks all flowing through the store. We sit in the snack bar and drink beer, careful not to spill on our clean floors. Rhonda sits up close to me, the way all the girlfriends do, as if they can't get enough of being close. A couple times I see Rhonda staring at the swelling in the front of Lisa's dress, and I know she is thinking about wanting to try again. The thought of it seems impossible to me, and for a minute I'm afraid—afraid that Rhonda is moving on, getting past this without me.

After everyone is nicely buzzed, Wilson suggests a game of hide-and-seek, while some of the others start riding bikes around the store. I find a public radio station playing Irish music, and I try to pull Rhonda out onto the floor, to show off the moves we've learned. She resists.

"C'mon, Curt," everyone shouts. "Hide-and-seek."

I look at Rhonda and shrug, then go to the breaker panel in the stockroom and snap off the lights. I leave the power on to the appliance department, so that out in the store the only light is the faint blue glow of the TV sets. The Irish music echoes across the store while everybody runs off to hide.

"Hey, you're it, Curt," Carlos shouts back at me. Rhonda puts her arm around me.

"I'll be it with you," she says.

"I'm no good at this," I shout across the store. "Give me a hint."

All is quiet, except for the fiddles and flutes of the music playing, a faint static hiss. The store in the dark seems huge and empty. Here and there I hear the suppressed laughs of Lisa or Tammy, one of them out there in the dim aisles. Soon, a bike horn honks, echoing across from the sporting goods department.

"There's your hint," Wilson shouts, and everyone laughs. Soon the others pick up the joke, and we hear the electronic *beep* of a talking book from the toy department, a rubber duck squeak from infants, the bike horn again, louder and faster this time. Rattles shake, pop guns pop, a bell rings, a toy piano, a

Talking Elmo . . . all these noises, all at once, like, I think, the ghosts of children, playing invisibly through the empty store. Then I am holding Rhonda as if to crush her.

"We don't have to look," she says. "Baby, we don't have to." She turns me a little, in time with the music, pushing my hands into place.

"Come on, dance with me," she says. "Balance and swing. We need the practice." The music is a fast reel, and I pick up the pace of it, twirling her faster and faster in the dark, pivoting on my foot. I try to think of all that Phil told us, all his empty cheer. I try to put my weight into the spinning of it, the way he showed us, closing my eyes and leaning back, feeling Rhonda do the same. The sounds of the bike horns and bells and rattles and toys grow louder; they are shouting to us, impatient for us to come find them.

"Keep going," Rhonda says. "Give me your weight. Go ahead. Give it."

Another Perfect Catastrophe

rodeo tricks

We're cruising down Dickson Street in the ragged vinyl buckets of my Pinto, and Sugar is chattering around a mouthful of peaches, telling me I'd better back up, he has just spotted a beret. I keep driving.

"Reed, you *have* to stop," he says. "Think of Bobby Seale, Sergeant Barry Sadler. Hey, Pablo *Picasso,* man." He tosses his fruit cup out the window, steals a Camel off the dash. "You saw it, right?" he says. I nod, sigh, pull over, and brake. Already he is hovering at low-middle on my happy-with-him gauge because he has again made us late picking up Lyndsey at the Hen House, and the back wheels of my Pinto are scraping from the weight of the acetylene tanks he buys to make more of his large, homely sculptures. His words, not mine—he likes to say he is of the large-homely school. He welds the sculptures without ceasing,

47

finishes one and starts the next, lets them rust away in the basement, in the attic, scattered around the yard.

So we're late and I'm torn because a feed cap is one thing,
but this one really is a French beret, dark blue and new looking,
which you have to admit is not something you see on the street
every damn day. So I back up, wait for traffic to thin. We sit
while the radio bounces out an old Donna Summer tune, then a
commercial for the Hairport. The road empties and I throttle
up again, hear the shush of wind and pavement as Sugar swings
open the door, leans out, and just beyond his knees the sidewalk
blurs past and he is yelling, "A little left, Reed, a little left," then
reaches and snags the beret, knuckles an inch from the asphalt.
Dirt and styrofoam whip around the floorboards. I ease back
into traffic.

"Man, we nailed that sonofabitch," he says, slams the door,
pries gum from the beret, and all I can see is Lyndsey and the
several ways she gets irritated, twirling her hair, shaking her
wrist so her watch slides down, chewing her lip. She is all about
promptness. She expects things to be on time. Sugar slaps dust
from the beret, tries it on. He tilts the rearview to check himself. Except for underwear, he never washes the clothes he finds
before he wears them, and thank God underwear is a rarity.
Mostly it is shoes, hats, T-shirts, the odd pair of pants. His latest
T-shirt, minus a sleeve, advertises the Page High Girls' Field
Hockey Team. The back says, GIRLS KICK BUTT! He found it
along Route 36, on the way home from the parts yard. He won't
drive because of his logging leg (he calls it), which has hobbled
him going on twelve years now. I don't mind, so Lyndsey minds
for both of us, but what she would never let herself admit is
that it was truly a righteous grab, that I never let the Pinto dip

under ten mph, that to someone watching we looked better than any rodeo trick rider, better than Tex Ritter or Monty Hale hauling a woman into the saddle. Lyndsey doesn't know these names. None of the movies she likes feature horses or gunplay.

I check my watch. "We missed Lyndsey," I say. "She's home by now and way pissed."

He fans his smoke out the window. "Hey, really, it's my bad, and I'll tell her that."

"I think she knows that, Sugar," I tell him. He nods, adjusts his beret. It covers the bald spot in his graying red hair.

"You need to marry that woman," he says. "All signs indicate that this is your last chance. And she's a good one, Reed, so don't blow it."

"I know," I say. The back wheels scrape. "I'm trying not to."

the generation gap

What I don't say is that *he* is the biggest chance that I will blow it. And you can't blame Lyndsey, can you? Sugar (his last name, his only name) and I are thirty-five, the both of us, Siamese twins joined at high school vandalism. Lyndsey is twenty-three, and I remember what that felt like, how you hit the exit door of state college and the ink on your diploma is still moist and you feel like you can step along the next forty-some years without the least stumble if only you are bright enough to avoid any deep woods and keep to the bread crumb trail that runs from your dorm room to the nursing home, about eight feet away. A few years will show you that the ones who tossed those crumbs ahead of you are only parents, bosses, teachers—all manner of fallible fuckups. But at twenty-three you don't know that yet. There's your generation gap, in ten words or less. Not the Lilith Fair or websites or nose piercings or sexual stamina or hair loss. Only that chasm in understanding. What else you don't know at twenty-three is that if you hurl yourself down that path, along the way all you will ever find is what everybody else has found before you, all you will see is a tree stump in a glass case, the rings labeled year by year.

At home Lyndsey is shoving chairs and a coffee table around the room, rearranging the house that Sugar's parents gave him when they retired to Puerto Rico. Last month she repainted everything. The house is out away from town down a dirt road, which is a good thing given the pipe bombs, but lately Lyndsey has been showing me photos of split levels and two-car garages in the weekly real-estate circular. Cul-de-sacs, planned communities, etc. She would like to have neighbors, bushes, fluoride in the water, backyard barbecues—all the normalcy she missed out on growing up. She shops for houses on the Internet.

Lyndsey has put the dog out in the yard, tethered to the clothesline, and I watch through the window while Sugar unloads his acetylene tanks and rolls on the grass with the dog in the cold and walks around looking at his latest sculpture, which he is making from tractor parts and the soup cans he blows into shards. He likes to blow things apart, then weld them back together, and this makes in those sculptures a kind of tension I like, even though I do not much care for midnight blasts and the balls of flame he sends into the treetops. The dog is a bloodhound named Ernest, who Sugar found and named (drunk, he will try to explain this) after *The Importance of Being Earnest,* saying that he didn't think Oscar Wilde would mind the borrowing or the misspelling, and that anyway Mr. Wilde shouldn't have taken the title as it would have been, with the altered spelling, perfect for Ernest Hemingway's autobiography, though I may be confusing the story—but somehow out of it all he managed to name a dog. He used to have a goldfish named Wuthering Heights, and a mynah bird named Absalom, Absalom.

The dog knows how to sniff out money, the way airport dogs can sniff drugs. Sugar bought a training manual and educated the dog to find greenbacks, paper money, and then he will turn him loose in the neighborhood and on a good day Ernest will bring home a few singles and sometimes a five or a ten, and we have no idea where he finds them, only that he is determined to find them and does. This for Lyndsey is exploitation, and she has a fervent sympathy for animals in the manner of all people who have at some time or another been gravely disappointed by human beings. When I met her she was VP of the local PETA chapter and even once stood with others downtown across from Vogel's Furs, naked under a blanket with a sign indicating she would rather be naked than wear fur, which would be my preference for her as well if you could separate the politics from the nakedness. Which of course you never can. We argued about this right after she moved in last August, and I took the position that training a dog to hunt money is not even in the neighborhood with meat eating and fur wearing, but when you are a twenty-three-year-old graduate student in finance, your thirty-five-year-old construction supervisor boyfriend is pretty much wrong on everything. So we avoid the subject. I do love her.

It has grown cold, early November, and I head out with Lyndsey to split wood in the backyard. Sugar is under the carport, his torch fired up and sending down a waterfall of orange and white. He limps as he walks around the sculpture, looking for the next place to spot weld a fragment of soup can. Lyndsey has on one of my old flannels over her blue jeans, with leather gloves cinched tight around her wrists. The girl can cut some wood, keeps her hair tied back. If you ever want to fall in re-love with your POSSLQ, let her wear flannel and do hard work. I watch her a while, stack the wood, take the sledge and wedge when she tires and we trade. Sugar hammers on his sculpture, the sound ringing through the cold.

"You pretty much trust him, don't you?" Lyndsey says. She wipes sweat from her face with her sleeve.

"What do you mean?" I say, though I know exactly where she's headed with this.

"Well, he's over there using a hammer, a torch. He isn't setting himself on fire, he isn't getting killed."

"Thanks for the update."

"You don't have to take care of him, Reed."

"I know that."

"You do and you don't. I think you feel guilty about him, and you know that's not healthy."

When she starts using words like "healthy," it's usually time to let the argument drop. I swing the sledge, miss, say nothing.

"We could move out of here and you'd still be his friend. I would, too. We don't have to *stay* here."

I swing again, lay the wood open and wet. "Listen, I like living here. We don't pay any rent. Sugar is a good guy." I shrug. If you want your language to fail, try explaining your male friends to your female mate.

"What is it you *do* all day with him? I mean, besides dig clothes out of trash Dumpsters?" I work only six months of the year, during heavy construction season. The rest of that time is downtime, nothing time, which I would not trade for anything. "The street," I tell her. "Sugar would never go diving some Dumpster. He says that fate hands him his wardrobe." She knows all of this and only uses reminding as a way of shaming me with the details. When she first met Sugar she went right along, saying that he made her laugh. Sugar has always been like a big toy, and when the batteries finally go, most are done with him. He gets old, Sugar does.

"Yeah, fate hands him most everything else, too," Lyndsey says. She adjusts her bra strap. "You're both too young to just quit your lives."

Sugar leaves his carport and starts walking around the yard, within earshot. We fall quiet, but I know this argument has only gone underground for a while. Sugar has his welding helmet tipped open and is walking around in circles, studying the ground as though surveying it. Say what you like, the boy *does* have plans in his head.

He walks over toward us, smiles at Lyndsey. She used to say he was handsome before his bothersomeness erased it. The welding helmet hangs over his face like part of some bird costume. The helmet when he found it (on Industrial Boulevard, leaning against a mattress) was missing its dark eye guard, so Sugar glued in a square of blue plastic cut from a soda bottle. The plastic leaves his vision wavered, like standing in the deep end, but he claims this makes for good sculpture.

I motion toward the carport. "What're you working on?" I know the answer already.

He shrugs. The helmet falls down and he pushes it up again. "New sculpture. *A Perfect Catastrophe,* I call it."

I grin at him. This is an old joke. All of his sculptures, since the start, have had the same title, only with different numbers.

"Another *Perfect Catastrophe*," I say. "I've lost count."

"Fifty-seven," he says. Lyndsey looks back and forth between us as if we are speaking in some elaborate code, which, I guess, we are.

"Hey, Reed, I need lumber," Sugar says. "I mean, I ordered some and need to go get it. I need a ride."

Lyndsey turns and shoots me a look, one of those little signals of anger or lust that will make of us finally a couple.

"How soon?" I ask him.

He laughs. "Hey, it's like that old joke, you know, guy says I need a board, salesman says how long, guy says a long time, I'm building a house."

I laugh with him, at the joke and at the way he compresses every joke, his life, everything in it compressed, hurrying toward nothing.

economics 101

That night in the bedroom, Lyndsey practices tai chi. She does Needle at Sea Bottom and Waving Hands Like Clouds. This relaxes her and focuses her both, she says, much the way TV and beer does me. I do Remote Control and Doritos while I watch her. I hate to be predictable, but I go with what works. On Friday nights I watch Lyndsey on the eleven o'clock news, when she does the Wall Street Wrap-up, three minutes of local stocks and investing tips sandwiched between the weather and sports. I like how she seems on TV, so distant and so much there all at once. I like how dressed up she is, her hair and makeup done, and how smart, talking all of us through graphics of the Dow and NASDAQ. She gave me another little signal to watch for, and some Fridays (not every) just when she says, "Back over to you, Bill," she gives a little twitch of a smile and then her full-kilowatt blast right behind it. Wouldn't see the twitch if you weren't looking for it. That little gesture is for me, to say that she is thinking about me and loves me, right there with the camera and half the town eyeing her. I bend close to the TV every Friday to watch, and if she does it, I shout like I have just won the state lottery.

Right now she's moving in slow motion, doing White Crane Spreads Wings. She is half-naked as she practices, wearing blue sweatpants, her hair still wet from the shower. She told me once that she is locating her internal self, her centeredness, that tai chi means "the grand ultimate fist." I wonder at this, how she finds her center by making her insides a fist. She grew up with a father who lost jobs the way other people lose car keys, and a mother convicted eighteen times for shoplifting. I would make my innards a fist, too, I think.

I watch her in the dark, lit by the blue of the TV, her nakedness in the cold light, her slow movements like storm clouds in a nature film. She hates the TV, but right now it renders her beautiful. After finishing with Fair Lady Works at Shuttles, she sits on the bed beside my knees, points the remote at the wall behind me, and turns off the tube, a decent bank shot. She clicks on the light. We are about to talk.

"We need to talk," she says. From atop her computer she lifts one of the green ledger books she uses in her investment management course, opens it across the bed.

"Here's the plan, Reed. If we move out of here, into some student ghetto until I graduate, then we pay out three hundred a month that we aren't paying now."

I nod, look at her. "Three hundred in the hole. Okay."

"But—" She kneels across from me. "If we're near campus, we cut out my commuting costs, and you are closer to town. We don't have to drive Sugar anywhere at all, and we don't have to pay for his food. Conservatively, this saves us maybe a hundred and fifty."

"But still in the hole," I tell her.

"Right, but what do we get for our hundred and fifty? We get us, honey. We get to *be* with each other, instead of tiptoeing around and acting polite and making sure we have on our bathrobes."

As she says this, I look down at the rows of credits and debits written in blue ink in her neat hand, then upward, at the way the wet tips of her hair sway and lightly brush her nipples. All in all, it's a convincing argument.

"I've lived here a long time, Lyndsey. Eleven years is a long time."

She takes my hands, knee walks over her own ledger book as she moves forward to straddle my thighs.

"Listen," she whispers, "you aren't doing him any good by staying here. He needs to find something else. His own life, maybe, instead of just tagging along with yours. You don't have to stay."

"Yeah, but what's wrong with staying? We have privacy."

"I would just like a little *normalcy* for once, Reed."

I start to speak, then we both jump as Sugar detonates another pipe bomb from the backyard. Orange light bursts against the curtain a half second before the explosion rattles my keys on the dresser. The shards of soup can clatter on the driveway. Lyndsey closes her eyes, draws steady breaths through her nose. I squeeze her hand.

"Let me think about it," I say.

She nods. "Better think hard."

how we met

Friday nights at the Hen House and all-you-can-eat crab legs. Snow crab legs, and Sugar wanted to eat them in the snow, in February, and Lyndsey was our waitress ten Fridays running, and slowly became a shared joke, a persistent glance, a nudge in the ribs from Sugar. We were two men just off from work (well, me), tired, doughy enough to be harmless. We asked her one night in early spring and she went with us, riding. Her T-shirt had a cartoon of a hen with a fishing pole, reeling in a big cat-fish. She wore black shorts. Gave her my denim coat to wear in the Pinto with its bad heat, Sugar leaning up between the seats like our eight-year-old and we are on our way to Six Flags. We bought little pony bottles of beer along with handfuls of Ding Dongs and Slim Jims, and rode out to the golf course, across the parking lot, and right up onto the cart path beside the first tee, clicked the Pinto down to parking lights. "I don't know about this, guys," she kept saying, and I drove slowly to reassure her, the cinders crunching beneath us, careful to stay on the path and not dig any tire ruts on the fairways. We handed our empties to Sugar and he placed them back in the carton. After a bit, Lyndsey settled into it, saying we were the most cautious vandals she'd ever seen. I liked the sound of her voice in the dark, the way her hair smelled like hush puppies.

Near dawn, the sky just edging toward light, we parked atop a hill beside the fourteenth green. Below us was the dark gape of a pond, the surface puckered by fish going after mosquitoes. Dew settled over the Pinto so that every few minutes I had to run the wipers. It was not yet sunrise, though there was a little rag of gray in the corner of the night, and the trees and yellow flags began to shape themselves. We got out of the car, walked to the edge of the hill in the wet grass, and below us the town lay spread out in darkness, the arc lamps strung like pearls through the streets. Light in the sky shifted again and all in one moment the streetlights blinked out, as if the town were giving in to daylight. "Wait till you see this," I told Lyndsey, and I watched her watching the town. "One more minute," Sugar said, and we were quiet.

Right below, a few hundred yards under our shoes, was the John Deere plant, and when the light in the sky notched up again, the green and yellow of those tractors bloomed into being like a sudden field of dandelions, and I took Lyndsey's chin and angled it down for her to see, the way Sugar did me the first time up there. Seventy-seven of them—tractors, harvesters, combines, backhoes, excavators—parked in rows on a wide gravel lot. Always seventy-seven, we had noticed through the years, so much so that we had stopped counting and went by faith. Dew glistened on the shiny green paint, the shadows of the machinery angled left in their own neat gray rows.

"Oh my God," Lyndsey whispered. She took my hand, then Sugar's.

I squeezed. "Like it?"

She nodded. "So beautiful. Like a Zen rock garden."

"With internal combustion," Sugar said. We stood silent and watching, as if we might see the little shift as the sun lifted over the hills and the shadows darkened and narrowed beneath the rows of machinery, as the town began to ripple with cars and noise. Then the sprinklers spread out over the fairways rose out of the ground and began spewing water in tapered arcs, and somewhere we heard a lawnmower start up.

"We'd better get moving," I said.

As we drove along the cinder paths, Lyndsey unpinned her nametag from her Hen House shirt and stuck it into my dash, left it there.

"I want to come back," she said. "I want to see that again."

why she stays

I don't know.

logging leg

It was something to do, road trip up to Oregon for a summer, escape the worst of North Carolina heat and no money. We were twenty-three, same age Lyndsey is now. We signed on with Hennesy Forestry Management Inc. for six bucks an hour, plus free lunch off the back of the silver truck at the foot of the logging road. We spent our nights in bars, chalking games of dominoes on the tables, trading money for half a buzz and a few jukebox dances with the local women, pretending that a pair of narrow beds and long hours of work equaled adventure. During the days we worked the skid trail, chainsawing the downed trees into eight-foot lengths, walking across the rows of logs under a high, dark canopy, with everything—the air, the logs, the ground—soaked with moisture. Sugar worked as a ballhooter, stepping across the logs, pushing them with a pole hook into neat bundles. After two days we could work in silence, the best way, speaking with only our eyes and nods of the head. The trees columned upward under a sky dark gray and marbled, the ground under our toe spikes needled, leaved, soft.

One late afternoon, a Thursday, I motioned Gil to back up the tractor to a bundle of logs and guided the winch while Sugar stepped across and looped the choker cable around the bundle. He looked at me to hit the winch as the motor started grinding. I stepped back with a pole hook to guide the bundle into place and as I moved away I watched the rubber bindings on Sugar's right boot come unstrapped, the spikes left behind, stuck in the log, and his right foot slipping down inside the choker just as the winch gathered the cable into its slow tightening. I looked at him as if seeing him there would tell me that nothing this wrong could possibly be happening, and his eyes held me, his mouth open and words splitting out of him as I moved toward the winch to hit the shutoff and saw the cable pull slowly through his jeans just above his knee as his other leg bicycled against the stack of wood and noise poured from his mouth, his hands grabbing at nothing, and the cable insisted its way into his flesh and I heard his bones as my hand found the red button and Gil, white-faced, exited the truck and clicked on his walkie-talkie. I didn't move, could not move. Sugar's eyes held me. My own eyes, still new to this silent language of work, found no words to give him, and I looked away.

the tough questions

"Why are we still together?" I ask. Lyndsey is readying for the Hen House, and I watch her slip on a T-shirt, zipper her skirt. "I mean, why are you with me?"

She sighs. "How did you get this old and stay this dumb?"

I shrug. "Easiest thing I ever did."

She shakes her head, pulls on her Hen House sweatshirt. If she follows her plans, in two years she will be making four times what I make now. "Because I love you, Reed. The oldest reason there ever was."

"But why?"

"You aren't supposed to ask why about love. You're supposed to let it stay a mystery. That's the rule."

I nod and watch her clip her hair up to keep it out of the catfish filets and cole slaw. "Love isn't such a mystery, really."

She cuts her eyes at me. "No?"

"Not for me." I shrug again. "A soft, warm body, a bed where we talk in the dark, your little TV smile on Friday night. Where's the big mystery?"

She shakes her head, frowns. "Well, that's shallow of you."

I know that she is no great believer in mystery, either, that this is just something you say about love when you are twenty-three years old. Her parents held little love but more mystery than

most see in a lifetime, a dad shedding jobs almost weekly, a
steady march of repossessors, and a mother who could not stop
stealing eye makeup or cans of soup or 45s from the record store.
Lyndsey turned away from all of that, left it for good at sixteen,
and now every step of her existence is planned out—career, vacations, the life she wants with me. She left mystery a long time
ago and has not looked back.

I look at her. "Why shallow? Who says love can't be made up of
real things? If there is any mystery, then that's it; there isn't any."

She walks over, takes my chin in her fingers. "Try as hard as
you can to make sense."

"Listen, you wonder about how we spend our days, let me
tell you. A couple months ago I took Sugar out to a work site for
copper scraps, and one of the guys on the crew stole his friend's
bag of Cheetos, just goofing around, and nailed it to the top of
a frame post. Then all afternoon we sat and watched these two
crows swoop down and land, pluck a Cheeto from the bag, and
fly off with it. One by one, until it was empty."

She smiles. "That's pretty cool."

"The point is, Cheetos and crows are just things. But you can
love them for themselves. What's wrong with just loving the
thinginess of things? They don't have to *mean*."

She leans down, kisses my upper lip. "Like those tractors on
the golf course."

I nod. What I don't say is that it was Sugar who first showed
me the tractors, Sugar who made a dozen guys stop a day's work
and sit in the shade to watch crows. Sugar is all mystery, and
there is, I think, no solving him.

She ties her hair back. "Listen, pick me up at midnight, okay?"

"Okay."

"And bring Sugar with you. We'll go ride, just like old times. It'll make us all feel better. We'll see some thingy things."

"You're too young to have any old times," I say. She gives me a look. "Okay, Sugar and me, things, midnight."

the old times

Before we leave that night, I find Sugar in the backyard, smoking cigarettes in the cold, hammering nails.

"Where's the torch?" I ask him.

"Not tonight. Other plans. A wedding present, actually."

He is pounding two-by-sixes together into a big square. He tacks angle irons into the corners.

"Wedding present for who?" I say.

"For you, Reed, who else?"

"So I'm getting married? This is news to me, buddy."

He motions me to help, and we place the square of boards on an even spot in the backyard. Sugar tosses a plastic tarp across it. "I have eyes and ears both, Reed. Don't tell me you aren't getting married. And you should, right?"

"That's my understanding, though I may have missed something." He hands me a staple gun and we walk around opposite sides of the wood frame, tacking the blue tarp to the boards. Above us the moon is thin and cold, the sky metal black. I feel sweat freeze in the hairs of my beard.

"Come on with me," I tell him. "Lyndsey wants to go for a ride. Like old times, she says."

He grins. "She isn't old enough—"

"I know, I told her that."

Ernest is watching us, his head lolling out of the doghouse Sugar made him from a yellow fertilizer barrel. Sugar finishes stapling and lays a bead of caulk over the staples.

"It's a little nippy for caulking," I tell him. He shrugs, says it will set eventually. He rubs his logging leg, which always bothers him more in the cold. We are quiet a minute.

"You ever think about it?" I glance down at his hand rubbing the knot on the side of his leg. "I mean, remember it?"

He peels caulk off his fingers. "I got three roommates, Reed. You, Lyndsey, and that memory. Every morning I wake up, it's there at the breakfast table eating Cap'n Crunch."

I nod, take a breath. "I didn't do everything I could have then. You know? I didn't . . . act." We stand together, looking at the tarp-covered box in the middle of the yard.

"What was there to do, a thing like that?" He shrugs. "A long time ago, Reed. I never held you to any blame. Things go the way they go."

The tarp ripples in a cold wind. Sugar picks up his welding helmet and puts it on, tips the mask up.

"You gonna tell me what this is?" I ask him. "Another *Perfect Catastrophe?*"

He smiles. "For a wedding present? Not a chance." While I am warming the Pinto, I see him with the garden hose pointed at this thing he has just built, as if he is washing off the plastic tarp, washing away all his hard work.

We get Lyndsey on time this go around, and have already been to the 421 for pony beers and Slim Jims and Ding Dongs. We find our way to Green Valley Golf Course and find the cart paths chained off, a security guard's car parked next to the club-house.

"Well, damn," Sugar says. "Somebody ruined it for us."

"Where to?" I ask.

"Just drive around," Sugar says. "Cruise and eat and drink."

Lyndsey shakes her head. "I don't want to just drive around all night." Her Hen House pin is still in my dash, where she stuck it five months ago.

"Why not?" Sugar says.

"I know a place," I tell them.

I drive us over to the giant parking lot behind Burlington Industries, where in the summer the tennis hacks line up to pound balls against the concrete slab at the back of the lot. We scale the wall from its tapered end and sit in the high middle of it, our legs dangling, asphalt twenty feet below us. Behind us is the big steel-and-glass building with its fountain spewing water up past the fourth floor. We are nearing Christmas, and the white lights in the fountain have been replaced by red and green ones, the mist blowing off the fountain, holding the color for a second, then vanishing into darkness.

Lyndsey wraps a blanket around her legs and scoots close to me, the hood of her coat edging her face with fake fur. We pass the little bottles of beer and fire up foul-smelling Swisher Sweets and sit in the cold drinking and smoking, not talking, Sugar pushing the mask of his welding helmet up and down so that the hinges squeak.

"You ever think about doormen?" Sugar says. He says this from behind the mask, his voice muffled. "I mean, it's weird. Say you're at that job for forty years. That is forty years of doing a single thing eight hours a day: opening and closing that one door."

I nod. "Yeah, strange. After so much time you must develop a relationship with that door. You know how many seconds it takes to swing closed, how much it weighs, what it smells like, where all the little nicks are in the wood." I feel Lyndsey shivering beside me. She finishes her second beer and opens a third, reaches for my cigar and holds it in her mittened hand, puffing and coughing, like a cartoon of someone smoking. Sugar is not done with doormen yet.

"I mean," he says, "that would be the worst part, that after you're seventy years old you look back and that's what you can say about your life. 'Well, I opened that door a lot.' Like, that's the whole ball of wax. That would be death to me, a job like that."

"At least it's a job," Lyndsey says. "At least you know what you're doing the next day." I give her hand a squeeze, open another beer.

"What would be the worst way to die?" I ask them. "Aside from being a doorman, I mean. I vote drowning."

"No *way*," Lyndsey says. "Burning up in a fire. Think how much a little arm burn on the toaster hurts."

"But it's quick," Sugar says. "The worst would be falling, like from a plane. All that time down and down and down, knowing what's coming, thinking about all the ways you fucked up."

"You wouldn't have time to think," Lyndsey says. "You'd be panicking."

I shake my head. "There is always time to think, no matter what."

"Hell, yes," Sugar says and tips up his mask. "Watch this." He stands up, wobbles, stretches his arms out, then jumps off the high wall toward the parking lot below, his loose jacket fluttering up behind him. Half a second later he lands on both feet and his mask clanks shut, then he limps around in a fast circle, saying, *damn damn damn* over and over, a fast little song.

"Nice going," I tell him. "You could've broken your stupid leg." He tips the mask up. "Just proving my point. All the way down, I thought about the pastrami sandwich I had for lunch."

Lyndsey lets out a sound that is half laugh, half disgust. "Yeah, and that's about as deep as your thinking would go, too." The way she shakes her head, I can tell she is drunk. With a small, thoughtless motion of her wrist, she throws down her beer bottle and it smashes on the pavement next to Sugar, pieces splintering across the asphalt. For a second, we are held in silence, as if waiting to see which way this moment will turn. Lyndsey looks at me, looks away.

"Missed me," Sugar says. His voice echoes around the parking lot, disappears up into the dark with the red and green mist behind us. He grins. "Strike one," he says. Lyndsey smiles at him, lifts another from the cardboard pack, and wings it out spinning into the dark, wind whistling at its neck. Sugar backs up, eyeing it, then snaps his neck so the welding mask swings down and he lets the bottle hit him full in the face, the glass shattering off the hard angles of the mask and spilling shards into his clothes.

"Man, oh man," Sugar says, voice muffled. "Again."

Lyndsey lifts, tosses, and Sugar leans back, letting the bottle hit and smash over him, a tiny popping sound, the pieces falling away from him as he moves.

"Reed, I kid you not," he says, "you have to try this."

I look at Lyndsey. "Go on, if you want to," she says.

I stand, jump, take the shock in my frozen legs. Sugar slips the mask over my head. It smells like copper pennies and sweat.

I tip up the mask, look at Lyndsey framed in the red and green mist. "Don't kill me," I tell her, and close the mask.

She smiles. "Make sure it hits the mask, not your head." She flings another bottle out against the sky and I watch it as far as I can and then at the last second close my eyes and hear it glance off the left side of the mask, skitter on the pavement.

"Good try," Sugar says.

"Not good," I say. "I cheated, blinked." I look at Lyndsey. "Again."

She takes careful aim on me, and the glint of the glass, her halo of fine hair, the mist behind her are all filtered blue, like I have found my own deep end. A brief knife glint of bottle in the night sky, a wave of indigo, then the *pop* against the faceplate and bits of light splintering around me like I am falling away from the world or being launched from it. Lyndsey waves in my vision, arm raised, and then she lets fly again in a line drive and I keep my eyes open, move my legs, let another bottle smash against the metal over my face and explode into stars, and behind me I hear Sugar cheering me, and Lyndsey stands at the edge of the wall with another bottle in hand, a girl who loves me, who wants to make her insides a fist, and as she flings and misses she bobbles, half a second, at the edge of that wall, and throws her arms up and out to catch back her balance and holds there, framed in a blue-white mist like some Orion or Cassiopeia seen through fog, and I know how much this girl needs *us,* as much as she wants only me. In Lyndsey's way of wanting, there will be no room for Sugar or bad parents, no accidental trips or falls, no mystery or blowing things apart—only a life as predictable as gravity.

This is not ancient history, not the days of chasing clothes along curb and gutter or the days of the logging leg and the nights of weary bones and the red button I could never quite push enough. This is Lyndsey, this is love blasted into shards that filter down through me. I lift the mask away and it squeaks and the cold pushes in behind it. I look up at her and she raises the next pony bottle and promises it will hurt plenty without the mask, swears at herself for almost falling, and I stop her cold.

"You want to get married?" The words bounce around the asphalt.

She looks. Blinks. Shrugs. "Do you?"

Sugar stands beside me, pulling glass out of my clothes. I nod at Lyndsey and slip the helmet off completely, back in this world. "Yeah," I tell her, "it sounds like a plan."

She sets the last empty in the carton, wraps her arms around herself. "Okay then."

Sugar takes back his helmet. "If you give the present," he says, "you create the event."

falling

That night we both fall into bed drunk and tired and cold, sleep arriving like some narcotic, and the last thing I hear before I give over to it is Sugar out in the backyard in twenty-degree weather, spraying the garden hose again.

By the next evening Lyndsey is freaked out because her eyes look like they should after the night we had, like they have been through a golfball washer, and she has the Wall Street Wrap-up at 11:17, right after Stu Nelson with weather. But she mixes in enough excitement about rings and dresses and honeymoon to let me know that last night has not been filed under "Too Many Ponies."

She kisses me and heads out. I sit watching TV, downing the odd aspirin or two. A little while later, Sugar walks out of the kitchen eating a powdered donut, his mouth ringed white. He hands me a shoebox, the ends duct taped. All day he has been in the carport hammering and welding, his face, even in this cold night, streaked with sweat. I open the box and find what look like two pairs of roller skates, the old skate-key type meant to tighten to your sneakers. Sugar lifts them from the box, the worn leather straps tangled, and turns them over to show me where he has removed the metal wheels and welded in a pair of thin, iron blades running parallel. Ice skates.

"Your wedding present," he says. "And that's not all. C'mon." He leads me to the backyard, where the tiny rink he has fashioned from the boards and plastic tarp lies shining under a half moon, the ice uneven and puckered along its surface.

He pulls a skate key from his jeans pocket and we sit in the frosted grass to try on the skates. The eleven o'clock news has started, and soon it will be time to go inside, sit on the couch, and watch for that little twitch of a smile from Lyndsey. But for now we take to the ice. The rink is only about ten feet square, and we push around in small circles like we are chasing each other, the iron blades scrapping up white ribbons of ice. Then Sugar grips my hand and we begin to whip each other around, turning faster, nearly falling, the whole table of ice rocking slightly on the uneven ground. The wind blows an eddy of old snow off the roof of the house. We skate around in the moonlight, breathing the cold air, hands slippery and damp, the silhouettes of all of Sugar's perfect catastrophes around us.

"I have to go soon," I tell him, out of breath. He nods, his face sweaty. Beneath us, the ice begins to crack from our weight, the underside shot through like shattered windshield glass. I think of breaking through into cold water, into the rush and press of a river, of how it would feel falling into all that blackness, the way it must have felt to Sugar in that moment when he knew that the log was no longer under his foot. But of course there is no river, no black water beneath us. The TV flickers blue against the curtains. Soon enough I will head inside to watch it, to warm up, to wait for her signal. The ice rink splinters, pieces of it sliding across the surface, the larger chunks tripping us. The boards are loose, pulling apart. We keep skating as long as we can, the dead grass of winter pushed flat underneath us, the black November sky above us. All around the moon, a pale ring of ice glows, promising more snow.

The Atomic Age

By eleven o'clock, almost all of the fluted glasses had been removed from the upper tiers of the champagne fountain and several from the lower, a trail of spills leading away from the garland-draped table. Jeremy Barseleau sat in a folding chair and watched the women in their heels and sequined dresses choose the amber glasses, silently urging them to take the lower ones, waiting for the removal of the one that would cause the whole thing to collapse. He'd earlier contributed to this effort himself, downing his sixth drink as the deputy mayor handed Jeremy's wife, Jean, an award from the museum for volunteer of the year. Applause had echoed off walls hung with enlarged photographs of microscopic animal life: tiny dust mites, deer ticks, and the mouth parts of fleas.

An elderly, overly rouged woman in pearls sat next to Jeremy, talking on and on about the battle of Fort Fisher and what heathens the Yankees were to attack on Christmas Day. He half listened, watching the pool of grease congeal around the meatball on his plate. At the front of the room, a man in a tuxedo and a light-up bow tie played requests on his portable keyboard. A large, plastic banner hung in the corner exhibiting his name, DON WEST, spelled out in fluid, Day-Glo letters. He passed around a cordless mike and asked everyone to help him out with "Jingle Bells," the crowd singing in noisy, off-key unison.

The woman touched Jeremy's wrist. "And your plans for the holidays?" she asked. Her mouth puckered downward at the corners, as though cinched. Jeremy glanced at her nametag, smeared by some food or drink she'd spilled. It looked as though her name were Kate—or had been, at least, earlier in the evening.

"Well, Kate," he said, "the usual, I suppose. I don't plan to attack anyone."

"Oh, heavens, let's hope not," she said, raising her hand to her thin chest. "You and your missus are traveling?" She glanced down at his wedding band. He looked at his own fingers as they twirled a fancy toothpick, the kind with the little colored plastic ribbon atop it. Somewhere, someone was making money selling plastic-topped toothpicks. The microphone passed him by.

"My wife wants to visit family in Florida," he said. "That's her, right over there." He pointed to where Jean stood, laughing and holding her Lucite statuette, the deputy mayor's hand perched inside the V of her backless dress. She looked gorgeous, as she had for as long as he could remember. Sometimes he saw her from a distance, for a moment not realizing it was she, and would catch himself checking out the roundness of her breasts or the angle of her hips.

"Your wife is Jean?" Kate said. "Volunteer of the year? Heavens, you must be proud as anything." She smiled, her dentures uniform and white.

"I am, Kate." He smiled back. "I'm proud of her." He told himself that this was what he felt now, pride, which somehow had learned to mock all the symptoms of boredom and fatigue. He loosened his tie and worked to undo the top button, which popped off and landed in his plate, a tiny satellite for the meatball. He listened as Don West segued from "Jingle Bell Rock" into "I Saw Mommy Kissing Santa Claus." These occasions seemed so easy for Jean, effortless. He supposed what he really felt was jealousy. The idea was silly—jealous of his wife for escorting preschoolers through the hydraulic dinosaur exhibit. Jealous of her donated time. Jeremy shook his head, poked at the meatball, pushed the button around in a helical orbit, drained the last of his wine. This was her third banquet in two months. She'd been named volunteer of the year here, and at the hospital as part of the Sunshine Patrol, and at the Red Cross as coordinator of their annual blood drive. The list stretched back over years. Jean did everything well for no money. He was mediocre and made enough to put them in a three-bedroom house with a detached garage and a pool. Aboveground, which he always felt didn't really count.

Jean moved toward him now, reaching out to friends as they passed by. He watched the sway of her spangled minidress, her smile as she approached. Kate had vacated her spot and edged over toward the dessert table, fragile in her heels. Jean placed the statuette in front of him.

"So what do you think?" she said. The Lucite was shaped like a flame, with her name etched into a brass plate at the base. The statuette was covered with the fingerprints of those who had passed it around to admire it. Jeremy picked it up and added his own prints.

"Nice award," he told her. She leaned against his table, her legs crossed at the ankle.

"How much could we get at a garage sale, you think?" Jean said. She waved at someone across his shoulder. Her mastery, he thought, extended even to her self-effacement.

"Well, there's not much market in used accolades," he said. "Congratulations anyway." He smiled and leaned up to kiss her cheek. She squeezed his hand and crouched next to his chair.

"You look like one of my dinosaur exhibits sitting here," she said, her voice quieter. "Boredasaurus once roamed the earth in a wool-blend suit."

"That's all right," he said. "At least if I'm extinct, I don't have to stick around for the macarena." He did a little dance in his chair. Above him, some microscopic parasite extended its pinchers in grainy black and white.

"I always thought you were a sucker for dance fads." She laughed, then lifted her hand to cover the tiny chip in her front tooth. She had gotten it in 1982, when a laundry delivery truck had edged out in front of them and Jeremy jammed on his brakes. The seat belts held them, but Jean's necklace, a large, silver seahorse on a chain, flew up and nicked her tooth. Sometimes it occurred to him that their whole collection of years was marked down in chips and tiny scars, the ghost lines of a few stitches.

He smiled and rubbed her arm. It pained him that he could not act better for these events, that he had lost over the years first his interest in her accomplishments and then his ability to feign interest. From various podiums, she always called him her greatest accomplishment, their twenty-one years together, and then as if it were scripted, the audience would smile and lean past their centerpieces to see him, and he would stand and wave to them as they applauded his existence. When the lights came up they would move toward him, toward Jean, in a steady parade of congratulations, as if their years were something else Jean had volunteered for, something else she'd managed well. And she had managed well, he knew. He thought of the Monday nights in spring and summer when they would sit outside on the deck so he could gaze through his binoculars at the night sky, watch lunar eclipses or the Perseid meteor shower, this ritual the last scrap of his boyhood interest in science. Not once had she ever revealed her own boredom with these nights, though she would always sit in the chaise lounge, her knees drawn up, trying to read by the glow of a book light.

They walked holding hands toward the anteroom for sheet cake and more champagne. Jeremy wobbled a little, startled as loud piano chords launched into "The Twelve Days of Christmas." Don West introduced the song by telling the crowd that the items in the twelve days added together would cost over eleven thousand dollars, assuming the rental fee for leaping lords. Everyone laughed.

Behind the long serving table stretched a display hall in dim light, featuring an exhibit on the history of flight in North Carolina. An oak propeller, slightly swaying, was suspended by fish line from the ceiling. In the back, a full-size single-engine airplane had been wedged next to the wall beside the water fountain, looking out of place on the orange carpet. Glass cases were filled with papers and drawings and photos, with the leather caps of flying aces. Two of the red letters were burned out on the EXIT sign above the stairway, so that the sign just read IT. Jeremy laughed.

"What's so funny?" Jean asked.

"First you're an it, then you're an ex-it," he said.

She squeezed his hand. "We're cutting you off right now. Drink water, mister."

"Ah, you better be nice to me," he whispered, slipping his arm around her waist. "One day you'll be an ex-it, too."

She looked up at him and half smiled, started to speak, and didn't.

"Have you seen this stuff?" he said, stepping around the table toward the aviation display.

"Honey, that area is closed for the night," Jean whispered.

"I'm just looking," he said. "Not going to hurt a thing." The only guard in the entire building was a small, plump blonde woman in an ill-fitting blue uniform, whom he'd seen standing on the first floor eating popcorn from a bag and watching the sparse traffic out the front windows.

"You are so bad," Jean said, but followed him.

They walked together past the display cases, looking at signed bicycle shop bills of the Wright brothers, old airline uniforms, grainy photos of long-buried heroes. When they reached the plane, Jeremy peered into the cramped cockpit, disappointed to see that the controls were only fakes, stickers mounted on black plywood. The left wing had been removed so the plane would fit up next to the wall. Jeremy snapped open the door, bent inside, and sat in the pilot's seat, straddling the stick.

"Where are you flying off to?" Jean said.

"I wish I had a good airplane story," he said. "Everybody I

know has one. Like, the landing gear wouldn't come down, or somebody got drunk and had to be restrained. Slid off the runway in the ice. One of those."

"I hope we don't have to restrain *you* before the night is over," Jean said.

"You *have* your airplane story," he told her. "The four-hour wait in Denver? Everyone traded ghost stories?"

She nodded and smiled. "I'd forgotten about that."

"Every flight I've ever had has been boring," he said. "I might as well have lived before they invented the damn thing." She leaned her arms on the windowsill, her face close to his. He looked at her, feeling almost cozy in this cramped space, wishing he had some reason to kiss her.

"Most people would consider a lifetime of boring flights lucky," she said.

"Then they don't appreciate the value of having something to tell. A little interesting noise to fill up the quiet."

She patted his arm. "This can be your airplane story."

"Doesn't count. We're not flying." He wrapped his fingers around the stick. "What did people talk about before we had traffic jams or airplane crashes or computer viruses or all this *stuff* in the world?"

She laughed a little and looked at him. "I don't know. You have other kinds of stories, don't you? Tell me one of those."

He held the stick and pulled hard right, as if banking into a steep turn, an evasive maneuver. Anything he could think of seemed redundant by its everydayness, as if the whole history of their years together amounted to no more than a shopping list or a weekend at the beach. Anything he could remember had been recounted again and again at reunions and in the shoebox of faded slides they kept beneath the bed. All the stories were birthdays and vacations and promotions and parties. They could have been written for anyone. He banked left.

"How about the time you got drunk at the museum and thought you were Snoopy?" She laughed again. "That will be your story."

He grinned at her and gave her a double thumbs-up to make her laugh more. This would be one of *her* stories, about him. Over the years, without meaning to, she had made him into her prop, a symbol of her stability. He heard her, at receptions and banquets, through the low hum of PA systems, chiseling him by her careful words into some kind of statue to her perseverance. Already, he knew, this story was hardening in some part of her mind. *A few onlookers behind us, his silly thumbs-up, he was drunk, acting like Snoopy.* No, not drunk; *tipsy* was a better word. She didn't want anyone to think he had problems. His legs started to ache. He pressed the rudder pedals and found they were welded into place. From the other room, Don West played a fanfare over the sound of champagne corks popping. He heard Jean's name called out. She looked over her shoulder.

"I better get back," she said. "You coming?"

He shook his head. "You go on."

Jean patted his arm. "Safe landing," she said as she walked away.

He watched the easy sway of her hips, the rhythm of her dress. She was, he knew, a very attractive woman and other men thought him lucky to be with her. He considered how his forty-three years of living had brought him to be half drunk and sitting in a crippled airplane watching his wife's well-maintained body as she walked out to be toasted by people who were strangers to him. This felt like the punch line to some elaborate joke.

Jeremy pulled himself from the cockpit, a sudden urgent fullness in his bladder. Downstairs by the coat racks, he remembered, they had passed a men's room on the way in. He headed out through the back hallway, the orange carpet dimly lit by track lighting, and came to an exhibit on the history of electricity. Glass cases displayed early lightbulbs and Edisonphones and lengths of copper wire. Outside one case was a plastic box with rows of green and red buttons. He pushed one, and a painted plywood panel lit up with tiny bulbs to show the path of lightning across the sky to the ground. He pushed another, and a man's recorded voice scratched through an overhead speaker, explaining the evolution of electrical generation and its importance to industry and the growth of America. Jeremy leaned close to the glass, watching the lights as the calming, neutral voice explained the history of power and man's harnessing of nature.

As he listened, his mind unearthed a glimmer from thirty years prior, ninth grade, when he'd attended football camp at Chapel Hill. He'd spent a week living in the dorm, sweating through his days in the damp air and dry grass of summer, running scrimmages and drills, drinking ice water from coolers. Near the end, the busloads of campers had come in early one afternoon as hard rains pounded the practice fields. They ran shouting from the buses toward the high-rise dorm. The fastest among them—a big, red-haired running back from Winston— sprinted to the door, laughing, his face streaked with mud, then grabbed the pull handle, spasmed once, and slammed to the concrete landing. He looked up blinking, as if he'd been lifted and thrown there. Others followed, their arms jerked by the force of the electric current that somehow had shorted out through the steel doorframe. They quickly discovered the pattern—everyone barefoot or grounded in cleats was jolted, and everyone in sneakers was not. They took turns, daring one another, letting the current snap their elbows.

Jeremy had held back until finally someone dared him. He hesitated, remembering stories about the electric chair and how the murderers' hair would smoke or their hearts explode. In the same instant he thought this, his palm touched the door, and something alive gathered inside his arm and ripped through his fingertips, the shock liquid and silvery. He heard profanity wrung from his own mouth and then stood looking at his tingling hand and the moment was over, his heart fluttering, the boys around him laughing. He and the others pulled on their wet sneakers and formed a line, holding hands, grabbing those who were barefoot or in cleats, each grounded touch sending the feathery shock through the long extension of themselves, adding to the line until there were nearly forty of them. They whipped around the asphalt lot like skaters, linked by their hands, tracking victims, the air metallic with the smell of ozone. The rain soaked his clothes, his arms pulled and twisted, rib cage aching as they ran shouting through the rows of buses and around the hedges that surrounded the building, his feet sometimes pulled off the pavement. For half an hour they ran after one another. He could see them now, like the tiny lights reflected behind the display glass, the years charged, old memory chasing him down.

Jeremy's hands slipped from the glass, leaving fingerprints and a greasy oval where his nose had been. He realized that they could have been, all of them, electrocuted. A wire-service tragedy, page-three irony. But that seemed now what gave the story its meaning, that they *hadn't* died and hadn't known that they could. More than anything else, reminiscence held all possibility of romance. Maybe the brochures for the museum ought to be rewritten to explain that this was all history was— understanding slathered on the messy past. The display lights blinked out and the taped voice ran quiet. He still had to pee.

The low thumps and vibrations of full-blown dancing sounded from the banquet room behind him. He moved along the dim halls and down a series of back stairs until he found the men's room. As he washed his hands, he looked at himself in the narrow mirror, his skin greenish and sickly in the fluorescent light. He patted his hair and hook shot his paper towel into the trash can. Near the elevator he found a still-smoldering cigarette in the ashtray and took a few drags from it, feeling it buzz inside his head.

Across the hall, an exhibit featured mannequins of pioneers posed near an orange plastic fire, holding cardboard skillets, coonskin caps perched crookedly on the heads of the men, the women in long dresses of rough fabric. The mannequins were the type on display in the hip, noisy stores of the mall— lithe and thin, their nipples erect. Jeremy laughed at this, then stepped over the Plexiglas partition that surrounded the exhibit. He straightened the caps of the two men, ran his finger along the fringe of their buckskin coats, hefted their rifles. The brown leaves under his feet were made of some thin synthetic cloth. He thought how it would look if he were to remain for the next school group passing through, how to explain the presence along the Oregon trail of a middle-aged section manager in a wool suit and argyle socks. He wore in his hair an oily formula meant to take away his gray. This was Jean's suggestion, that he lose the gray he thought he had earned. Jeremy decided that the fact that the hair color was her idea ought to be pointed out in the self-guided tour pamphlet. He posed for a moment, as still as his drunkenness would allow him, pretending to warm his hands over the orange cellophane. He looked at the men around him, their still, chipped faces.

"Looks like a hard winter ahead," he said, startling himself with the echo of his voice. He tried to imagine pioneer names for them, but could not think of any. As he ran through the list of the men he worked with, it amazed him how none of the names would fit: Stan, Rog, Anthony, Kevin, Stephan. Sissy, soft-handed names, he decided, then reached out and fingered the nipple of the pioneer woman through the gray fabric of her dress. She rocked a little on her stand.

"Can I help you, sir?" For a moment, he felt the jolt of the steel door passing through him again. He looked up to find the security guard shining a flashlight politely away from his face. She wore an oversize, shiny blue coat and blue uniform-store clothes, her ponytail looped through the plastic adjuster of her hat, which read SENTRY SECURITY in bright red letters. She chewed a wad of gum, her slight double chin appearing then disappearing.

"I'm with the party upstairs," Jeremy said. He moved past the fake campfire. "My wife . . ." He let his sentence trail off.

"That your wife?" She pointed the light at the pioneer mannequin. "She's a little old for you. Like, maybe a hundred years." There was no discernible humor in her voice, and the warmth of a blush slowly crept into his face. He felt clumsy, exposed. When he tried to laugh, the sound came out like a small choke.

This was something else Jean was good at, the tiny performances that brought one through a day of public living.

"I'm just . . . what can I tell you?" he said.

"Your name?" the woman asked.

Jeremy started to pull out his wallet. He straightened up as he always did in dealing with police at traffic stops, as if good posture could keep him out of trouble. His billfold opened to a row of credit cards.

"I don't care if you can *drive* or not," the woman told him. "I just want to know your name."

"It's Jeremy. Jeremy Barseleau. Yours?"

"Celina Di Felice. It's Italian, even though I don't look it."

"It's pretty, though, like a little song."

She nodded. "The same line you use on all the pioneer women." Her own small laugh sounded more like a sneeze. She motioned with the flashlight. "I guess my job is to tell you that you ought to come out of there."

"And miss the gold rush?" He laughed this time, but she did not join in. He had never really known how to make other people laugh. Somehow his timing was off.

She held his hand as he stepped over the Plexiglas, her grip cool and strong, her hand tiny and rough. He thought of Jean with her large, red-nailed hands. He tried to imagine her hands unadorned—empty, like this woman's, of color or jewelry.

He straightened his tie. "Thank you. Sorry for the trouble."

She shrugged. "Gave me something to do. You should have resisted so I could shoot you."

He smiled. "At least let me get you something to eat."

"They got food up there?" She clicked off her light, slipped it into her belt.

"I think they may have a little. About two banquet tables' worth."

She smiled, her teeth crooked and white. "If you insist. Get me some food and I won't arrest you."

"You can't arrest me. You are just a play cop, aren't you?"

"Well, you're just a play party guest. Otherwise you'd be upstairs. Who are you avoiding?"

By now, Jean would probably be looking for him. "I'll get your food," he said.

Upstairs, Jeremy loaded a plate with chicken wings, shrimp salad, canapés, a slice of brie, Watergate salad, and German chocolate cake. On the way down he grabbed two of the rib-boned champagne bottles that lined the stairs. He carried his load of food down to the pioneer display and found Celina gone. He shielded his eyes against the track lights to make out the covered wagon and the pioneer woman in the shadows. This was the place, but she was nowhere around.

"Celina?" he whispered as he made his way back through the dark halls, past old hay rakes and mattocks and plows, past colonial drawknives and rosin barrels. Almost without meaning to, he stopped briefly to look at each display. It awed him, how many things people had thought of to invent. He wondered if there were a limited supply, if someday there would be nothing else to make, nothing else to think of or know. He imagined people standing around looking at each other and shrugging.

He found a rear stairway and walked up, balancing the food and bottles. At the top was a steel door, though he could not remember which floor he was on. The door opened out behind the awards table, the unclaimed statuettes still scattered across it. Jean stood off a way, holding the unlit cigarette she kept with her in an attempt to quit. A small circle of friends surrounded her.

"Well, look at you!" she shouted. Jeremy walked over toward her. "There *is* plenty, honey, you don't have to hoard it." Her group laughed.

Jeremy stopped and held the load of food as if someone had dumped it in his arms. "I'm hungry, I guess."

She pointed her cigarette at the bottles. "Thirsty, too, looks like." He hated this time of the night, when after a few drinks she would draw laughs by teasing him, sketching their marriage by way of little jokes and asides. It was these nights when he could convince himself he was done with her, that their years had brought them to nothing. As he shifted the bottles under his arm, a bit of shrimp salad fell to the floor.

"Jeremy, listen," she said, pulling him to a safe distance. She spoke low into his ear, her voice losing its practiced lightness—more real now, more worried. What he wanted, he sometimes thought, was for the breezy, public Jean to be his all the time. For their marriage to be the way it seemed when he sat in folding chairs and heard her talk about it over the faint squeal of microphone feedback. He wanted to marry the woman behind the podium. She leaned on his arm.

"The mayor's dance is at midnight, and I would like you there to turn me around the floor." She fingered his wedding band. "I know these things aren't fun for you, but it's the one favor I'm asking. Please don't disappear on me."

"I'm just looking at some of the displays," he said. She smiled. She was really sweet, he knew. This was the consensus among their friends.

"See anything good?" she asked.

"I watched a show about the way teenagers ignore death," he said, "and I toured the hall of pioneer nipples."

A look of small panic crossed her face. He was talking too loud.

"You'll have to show me those sometime," she said.

He nodded. "I'd like to."

"Go easy on the champagne, and don't forget the dance, please, Jeremy. This really is important to me."

"Haven't I always been there when you needed me to?" This was a line he'd heard on a TV show somewhere. He stood close to her, speaking in a quieter voice.

"Yes, you have." She squeezed his arm. "Come find me."

"Midnight," he said. "Got it. Promise I'll be here." He thought drunkenly of Cinderella.

He felt his way down the back stairs by the faint red glow of the fire escape signs. His steps gave a hushed echo on the stair skids, the thick base of the champagne bottle tapping the handrail as he descended. He walked through the halls, calling for Celina in a hoarse whisper. He passed mannequins dressed as redcoats and as colonists with muskets and fake plastic horses, and others clothed as Rebels and Yankees. The set faces were lit from above, the clothes too new-looking, as if they had come from Wal-Mart. Jeremy fell into the habit of speaking to these figures as he passed, showing them the twenty-first-century miracle of his digital glow-in-the-dark wristwatch and his cell phone, asking if they had seen a blonde dressed as a cop. He told the plastic Yankees that they should not attack on Christmas Day.

Finally he found her, in a large room set aside for special visiting exhibits, the current one titled "The Atomic Age." Celina sat cross-legged on a love seat inside someone's re-created living room from 1955, watching Milton Berle on a boxy black-and-white TV. Outside the fake window was a bomb shelter shaped like a small RV, air vent jutting upward, one wall cut away and replaced with Plexiglas, the olive-drab shelves stacked with Wheatena biscuits, Ritz crackers, and steel cans of water. He sat beside her, the vinyl upholstery squeaking beneath him, the two of them surrounded on three sides as though they lived in some fourth-grader's diorama.

"You found me," Celina said, smiling. He handed her the food, spilling some on the beige carpeting. He felt clumsy, as if he somehow had failed her instead of doing her a favor. She lifted a forkful of Watergate salad to her mouth. He undid the foil and wire on the champagne and popped the cork. It ricocheted and landed on the end table, atop a copy of *Life* magazine with Dwight Eisenhower on the cover.

"You got him," she said. "I come down here to goof off. Don't tell."

"Who would I tell?" he said. "Hey, Uncle Miltie, see that she's fired." At this, she laughed out loud, as if he had finally hit some resonant spot. He watched her laugh, the way it just came out of her all at once. He decided that he loved this in her. On the tiny screen, Milton Berle was wearing a dress and trying to kiss Danny Kaye. The audience howled. Celina chewed, drank from the bottle, then passed it to him, and he drank. Nothing had ever tasted so good, and he drew long, fizzy swallows until his eyes watered. He saw her with clarity as his drunkenness increased, saw the small imperfections of her nose and the thin, hard lines around her mouth. She was almost pretty. Celina tipped her hat back on her head and leaned against the love seat, shutting her eyes against the lights. She stood up suddenly and changed the tape in the VCR hidden under the TV cabinet.

Jack Benny flickered onto the gray screen, frowning and holding his violin. Across the hall, in another room, Jeremy could see more of the enlarged photos of microscopic animals, the hairy legs and dangerous pinchers. It surprised him that such a small world could be so fierce.

Celina drank. "Where's wifey?" she asked. This annoyed him suddenly, her calling Jean "wifey," as if subtly mocking him for being married to her.

"My wife, Jean, is upstairs, being awarded and feted."

"Are you happily married? Or do you secretly hate it?"

He looked at her. There was a tiny smear of sauce on the corner of her mouth. "I know your type. You think it's smart to ask questions that put people on the spot."

She shrugged. "I hate small talk. Just another name for bullshit."

"To answer your question, I'm happy if I don't think about it too much. Married happiness is like, I don't know . . . an autonomic response."

"What's that mean?" she asked.

"Like your heart beating or your eyes blinking. You don't have to think about it."

"Or don't *get* to think about it," she told him. As she said this, he was hit by recognition: this was *their* old furniture, his and Jean's, or something very much like it, castoffs from his in-laws the first year they were married, when being poor felt like fun. He pictured their cramped apartment, the rusted, leaky toilet, the plumbing that would groan and honk in the middle of the night, and how in the dark, wedged together in their bed, he would make Jean laugh by telling her that Harpo Marx was trapped in the wall. He looked around, remembering the low-slung aqua-colored vinyl couch, the coffee table shaped vaguely like an artist's palette, the abstractly designed ceramic ashtrays. In the mock kitchen were a Formica table and chairs, metal cabinets painted bright yellow, and vintage Tupperware displaying a Jell-O mold and green bean casserole. Everything plastic, fake, more so even than it had been then. Preservation, he supposed, equaled history.

"My wife and I used to live here," he said. "Except we didn't have a bomb shelter."

Celina wiped her mouth. "You're kind of a quirky guy."

He shrugged. Jack Benny faded out and a commercial for Texaco came on the screen. "And what about you?" he said.

"I'm not that quirky."

He took a cracker from her plate and bit it. "But are you married?"

"I live with my boyfriend. He sells cars. He's learning to play the drums."

Jeremy nodded and looked at his watch. In twenty minutes the mayor's dance would start and Jean would be looking for him. He closed his eyes a moment, weighing the drunkenness inside him.

"Bored with me already, huh?" Celina said. "It's the job, not me. The boredom just clings to me."

"You're not boring," he said. "Do you plan to work this job all your life?"

"No," she said. "I want to be a nurse. Either that or euthanize dogs for a living."

He looked at her.

"I'm *joking*," she said. "Except about the nurse part. Lighten up, Jerry."

"Jeremy," he said. On the screen, Dr. Joyce Brothers stood locked in an isolation booth on *The $64,000 Question*. Out the window, surrounding their bomb shelter, stretched a lawn of bright green Astroturf.

"I hate all this phony newness of everything," Jeremy said.

"Hey, this stuff is fifty years old. Older than me by a mile."

"Old but new," Jeremy said.

"You want older, like antique?" Celina said. "Jerry wants to go back in time."

He drank, and she wiped his chin with her finger. "Isn't that what everybody wants?" he said.

"Not me, buddy. Nothing back there I want."

He grinned. "You're the here and now, huh?"

Celina drank from the champagne and handed it to him, then stood. "Come on," she told him. "You want old, I'll show you the off-limits stuff."

She led him out of the Atomic Age, through darkened halls and along back stairways, past a display on extinct mammals, past dugout canoes, mannequin conquistadors and explorers. They entered a door posted AUTHORIZED PERSONNEL ONLY. Inside, Celina skimmed her flashlight along a row of empty glass cases to the back of the room, where an artificial cave had been built against one wall. The outside was unfinished, the concrete and wire mesh and fiberglass exposed; the inside walls were textured and painted to look like limestone. Beneath Jeremy's hand the mouth of the cave felt like the real thing, a solid, permanent opening into the earth. Somewhere above them, he heard the shuffle and murmur of the party, the faint bass notes of Don West's keyboard.

"It's a new exhibit they're building on early man or

something," Celina said. "We aren't supposed to be here. At least, *you're* not."

It was approaching midnight. "I have to go soon," Jeremy said, slurring a little. Celina nodded. He undid his tie and stepped into the cave, imagining that the air felt cooler, damp. The cave was at least twenty feet deep, the back wall a black-painted sheet of plywood. He thought of the airplane with its fake controls.

"Where are the department store cave dwellers?" he asked.

"Still on order, I guess. All the mannequins come from either Indonesia or Pittsburgh."

"The two seedbeds of civilization." He stepped farther inside. On the floor were three metal plates where the mannequins would be bolted down.

"Kill the light," he told her. She shrugged and clicked the flashlight, the bulb wire a faint orange glow behind the lens. He heard the jingle of her keys, the squeak of her leather holster as she stepped over the ropes and toward him. Sounds came more fully to him now, the noise of the party upstairs muffled through a heating duct, carried along the currents of filtered air. His eyes pulsed in purple steaks and flashes against the dark. Celina's fingers brushed his wrist. She took hold of his sleeve.

"This is weird," she said. "I'm glad I'm not blind. I would hate that." Jeremy heard through the faint *whoosh* of air the sounds of spoons stirring in coffee cups, champagne glasses clinking, Don West playing slow, intermittent chords on his synthesizer and talking to the crowd. There was a short crackle of applause, then a burst of laughing like noise rising out of a radio speaker. The rough wall of the cave came up behind him as he felt his way, and he let himself slide down, sitting on the hard floor.

"Where are you?" Celina said. As his eyes adjusted, she became a faint, blue-white glow. "Can we sit? I'm tired."

"Here," he said, taking her hand. He could smell on her a faint odor of garlic mixed with the champagne. As he raised his hand to her, his wristwatch moved like a firefly in the dark cave, flashing 11:53. He pushed it up under his sleeve. The sounds of the party faded in and out, layers of laughing and dancing and music and silence. The air vent blew down on them, cooling their skin. It would be good to have a fire, he thought. Celina sat next to him, their shoulders touching.

"This is *so* cool," she said. "I can almost see you. Like I can, but only sorta, like a really faint star at night."

"You smell good," he told her. "You smell like food."

She laughed. "You just want everybody to like you, don't you?" she said. He heard her moving around, settling in.

"Same as anyone. That could be the theme of this entire museum. Except the dinosaurs and insects; they don't give a shit."

"I like you pretty good," she said. "You gave up a whole party to hang out with me." She patted his hand, groping a little to find it. Above him he heard different off-key singers trying drunken verses of "All I Want for Christmas," and he pictured the handheld mike making its way around the room, past his empty seat, Jean sitting, twisting her napkin, watching the stairwell doors. He spoke quickly.

"Ask me some more questions," he said. "Ask anything." He wanted to tell her every thought that came into his mind, as if by words he might make her understand who a Jeremy Barseleau is, who he had become in forty-three years.

"Hmmm." She was silent. "Tell me one time when something really broke your heart. Or someone." She leaned against him.

The question panicked him a little. He tried to think of Jean in some setting that had moved him deeply, brought him to real sadness. There was the time not long after their marriage, in a walk-in clinic at the hospital, when they were told they could not have children. But he could remember only the long first days of silences and averted glances that came after, how Jean had joked them out of themselves until through time the loss seemed only a mild disappointment, like a picnic rained out. Since then, it had never seemed that they really *needed* children. He ran through other things in his mind, old girlfriends, sad movies he might have seen, deaths of distant relatives, watching his parents as they aged. All of these things seemed remote now, fuzzy around their edges. Then he remembered something, and quickly turned to Celina.

"This will sound silly," he said.

"Yeah, probably so. Just try me."

"It's a little thing, really. Once, Jean and I were at this company picnic at Hagenstone Park. The usual, cooking burgers, swimming in the lake, volleyball. I was hot and sat under a tree and watched this other family, not part of our group." Jeremy shifted his legs. "This is stupid," he said.

She took his hand and squeezed it. "I don't care. Tell the story."

"Anyway, they were all doing the usual stuff, too, and the kids were bawling over fruit punch or something, and I saw what must have been an uncle, an overweight guy in tattoos and this mesh shirt and tinted glasses, he's away from everyone, with the family dog, some little mutt on a leash. The guy has the leash looped around his ankle and he's inside this narrow patch of shade trying to work this big corkscrew into the ground so he could tie up the dog."

Jeremy took a deep breath, feeling words gather in him. In the dim quiet echoed the sound of a synthesized fanfare upstairs, then the deep tones of the mayor's voice. He could feel Jean's waiting. Words spilled out of him.

"I just thought about him sweating, digging into the dirt, tearing up his back. The guy is slipping and puffing like he's going to have a heart attack, just so the dog could rest in the shade. I mean, a damn dog. It seemed like he had tied *himself* to the dog, not the other way around. No one even noticed the guy. No one helped him."

He stopped, his lungs filling. "I probably sound like a *Lassie* episode," he said. Applause filtered down to them, the mayor having finished his speech.

"I love that," Celina said. "I feel like I love that man."

Jeremy nodded. "It's weird. That's what I felt, too. Like he deserved something from me."

She turned toward him. "Well, now he has it. You told about him."

He wanted to tell her everything, about the man and the dog, about the electrified boys in the rain, all the small moments of his past. Beside him he could just make out the movements of Celina, her starchy clothes rustling like grass. He felt the weight of his drunkenness, allowing his head to tilt against her shoulder. From this angle he could see high on the opposite wall the faint, crude scratches of cave drawings, dark as rust at the edges of his vision. Upstairs, the keyboard started "One O'Clock

Jump," and feet shuffled across the floor above them, through the layers of insulation and particleboard and the concrete and fiberglass of the cave. He heard laughter, the faint wheeze of breath through Celina's nose, her fingers smoothing his hair.

"You'll be all right," she said. "Sleep it off."

He reached back behind him and found with his fingertips the indentations of other drawings, rough figures etched and painted into the stone, his hand careful as it traced the shallow lines, the thin, smoothed ruts. He heard his own name then, called in dim echoes, the laughing that followed it. He imagined Jean with the cordless mike, making a joke of looking for him, her voice altered and modulated, his name something far off and unrecognizable. The sound faded against the rushed pulse of his blood, the scant sigh of Celina's breathing. He held to the sound of his name as his fingers traced the jagged lines on the wall. He wondered what tales they told, of hunts or kills or defeats, and in what language they might be written, some ancient language lost to history, telling stories without words.

The Small Machine

George Bartel has earned enough money in commercial lending to finally afford an extravagance, and now finds himself seated on an airplane, muscle relaxants in his blood to forestall nervousness, his wife Maurya beside him. He liked the idea when it occurred to him, she loved it when he told her: three Valentine's Day dinners in three time zones, toasting twenty-two years of marriage across the continent. So romantic, she said, so expansive. They're due, he said. And so they began that afternoon in Boston, with orzo pasta and wild mushrooms, *fugasa* bread, and pear-and-hazelnut crisp, and now a three-hour hop to St. Louis for chicken with passion fruit and champagne, then on to San Francisco for Belgian waffles and mimosas. Roses and a limo ride started the night, sleepy handholding and familiar sex will end it. Two stones, they are, skipping across time and geography.

Like most plans, this one is already truncated, deformed. He's saved money buying coach and now sits with his knees scrunched, feet cramped. The air vent blows its staleness and stink. Every seat is full, babies crying in rounds, no one watching the mime show of flotation devices and oxygen masks. George's thighs hurt, and the prescription makes his heart race, his palms over dry, his scalp tingly. "This is *so* exciting," Maurya says, and, God bless her, means it. She is still pretty, despite the years that have pulled him down into jowliness and a measurable gut, despite the severity of her haircut, which, if she were a boy of ten, he would call a brush cut. Gold hoops dangle from her ears, swaying as she dabs nail polish at the run in her stockings.

The ground drops away as the prescription smears his usual quiet panic into an agreeable fog. The pasta has settled badly, and he hides a belch in his fist. The young woman in front of him (he noticed her when they boarded—a round, plain face and chunky calves, but that *hair,* a shiny curtain of it hanging several inches past the hem of her T-shirt) tips her seat in full recline, squeezing him. He sighs, too loud. Nine more hours and two more meals of this, the airliner gaining time he doesn't want. Maurya kisses his hand, an old gesture that still moves him. He decides to do better.

The captain comes on fuzzy through the speakers and tells them—George could swear he hears this—to eat their peas. The cart rattles down the aisle and he buys two tiny bottles of rum to mix with Coke, then accepts the foil packets of almonds and a cellophane packet of candy hearts, for Valentine's Day. Everything is whimsy now, the world laughing at its own jokes. Maurya reads some aloud as she feeds them to him: BE MINE. HOT STUFF. Air hisses through the fuselage, and the seat belt sign winks out.

The old, darkened NO SMOKING signs are still at the ready, should the latest tyrannies ever vanish from the world. Maurya asks if he's okay and he promises he is, speaking through the sugared paste on his tongue. He rinses with drink and thinks better of taking another pill, his palms still papery and dry.

Just as Maurya settles in with *People,* as George allows his eyes their heaviness, the young woman before him, stirring in half sleep, lifts her heavy hair from behind her and tosses it free of its confinement, her motion practiced and effortless. The hair fans out in slippery waves, a billowing of auburn, gold, saffron in slow motion, like a shampoo commercial. The bulk of it settles, thickly, in George's lap.

Maurya, engrossed in Mel Gibson and celebrity weddings, fails to notice. The hair, dense and opulent, slides along the folds of his wool slacks, cascading as he shifts. Night encloses the plane as the cabin lights darken, people napping on pillows or sitting under their spot lamps, quiet performers on a dozen tiny stages. In the shadows George lets his knuckles graze the tips of the woman's hair. Soft, a silk chemise, the fur of some exotic animal. Maurya slowly nods off, and George, emboldened, a little drunk, extends his fingers so the hair slides down between and through, the gold of his wedding ring a nugget in the bed of some coppery autumn stream. The young woman sleeps, her nose slightly whistling. He combs her tresses with his hands, bundles it loosely in his fist like bolts of voile, and admires its liquid falling. Then the woman shifts, stirs. George's heart whirs like a small machine. He closes his eyes, then thinks better of it, imagining Maurya waking and finding him, with half an erection, touching one of the other passengers. He holds her hair and bends to sniff it, careful of his movements, pretending to adjust his socks. The smell is honeyed, ambrosial . . .

The woman sits up.

He drops the hair and adopts good posture, snatches a safety folder from the seat back and opens it. With feined concentration he studies the cartoon drawings of faceless, androgynous passengers escaping down an inflated slide. The woman turns, blinks, looks at him without accusation. He smiles, and she settles back again.

Hands shaking, he flips the safety card to a map of the airline's hubs, red dots spread across the country, a disease. The map is made of colors: red for Eastern Time, blue for Central, yellow for Mountain, green . . . He looks again at that boxy yellow swatch, the jaundiced middle. Somehow, he's forgotten Mountain. For weeks he's bragged about his plans, and no one asked about Idaho or Montana. The travel agent never brought it up. Even the TV neglects Mountain. Every night, the announcer speaks only of Eastern, Central, and "later on the West Coast." Not one word about Mountain, that yellowed hole in his plans. The entire scheme seems pointless now, riddled with faulty plans and superfluous time zones. Even the woman's hair is probably some kind of ruse—a wig, maybe, or expensive chemicals purchased at a salon. He reaches up again, lets his fingers slide through the soft strands, remembering the experience of finding beauty there as though it had happened years ago and not two minutes prior.

How wrong can he be? First the trip and now the hair, all his feeble desires filtered through his own candied heart. He lifts her hair again in both hands. The smell is the thing, all the old nostalgias. Grimsley High, class of 1972—cheerleaders and backseats and sweat and promise and ache. The captain announces their arrival time, the hour shedding minutes to the swiftness of the plane, and George shedding years to the swiftness of his life. He presses his nose into the handful of hair, breathing. Why had they made this trip at all? The full implement of love became operational at age sixteen; the rest was only packaging, bright distraction from rust and wear. His entire plan feels arbitrary, fake, set up, the whole idea of Valentine's Day nothing more than some corporate contrivance, propped up by Hallmark and Whitman's. He knows how the world works. The grown-up world of falseness and whimsy. He holds the fan of hair to his face. They should have stayed home, bought a porch swing. Built a porch. Sat and held hands. If not that, not in their own mortgaged space, then what is there to find in St. Louis or San Francisco?

George breathes deeply, fighting tears, rubbing the hair into his eye sockets. He imagines this: a wife, a husband, swinging out and then back into the comforting drop he feels now as the plane begins its slow descent, swinging out over the night and the neighborhood, the welcoming blue-beaded landing lights below no more than the straight lines of TV sets, guiding them to ground, easing them out of the dark. He releases the bundle of hair and sits back, Maurya stirring, muttering in her sleep, settling against him. His feet push against the narrow carpet, moving Maurya lightly in her sleep, his fingers finding her severe hair, stiff with mousse. He moves his fingertips, over and over, soothing her, each tiny hair a needle of compunction, steely and familiar.

19 Amenities

We are not big time, and as Tricia says, it takes no lethal act of imagination to see that. Here is how bad it gets: About sixty miles outside Jacksonville we were cruising high because Tricia's Blitz made his best showing all winter, coming from the outside eight box on a muddy track and placing second in the sprint stake, winning enough to get us motoring back toward West Memphis, tossing leers at one another, sharing little airline brandy bottles in the front seat with Tricia edged close to me and her hand on my thigh. Near dark we stop for burgers etc. at a Tastee-Freez and then get back in the station wagon and the horn and dome light stick. I mean they won't quit this blare of noise and light until I pop the hood to yank the ground wire, then claw at the headliner and start shearing wires with Tricia's nail cutters. After that it's two hundred miles of dark, with no light for bathroom

breaks or road maps, no horn if we start to get killed, and that
flap of headliner waving between our heads like some don't-
get-horny warning flag. Highway 10 is a bad pull of road like
this, the Delta scary quiet, the Gulf Coast just another something to get past; and like he knows things are going to shit, Tricia's Blitz whines and scratches at his crate, and we have
nothing to feed him but pork rinds we buy off gas-station racks.
The plan is to hit the winter races at Texarkana, then swing back
through West Memphis, but the thing about no dome light is
that every plan looks worse in the dark.

While my brain grinds through this current run of badness,
Tricia walks out of the shower with a towel tucked around her
breasts and another around her neck like a boxer. This is the thing
about motels, for a few days you are rich in towels. We are on the
second floor because Tricia believes that mice can't climb, that
roaches are fearful of heights. I like this towel business, and Tricia all dewy from the shower, her face deep pink from a half
hour in the exercise room, which in this kind of place is only a
duct-taped bench and a weight bar, plus one of those bikes with
a big box fan where the wheel should be. Tricia has been working on her pecs because, she says, they are in cahoots with her
breasts, which are starting to give her worry. They are learning
all they need to know about gravity, she tells me. She is forty-
three and expert at fretting. And from Texas, where she used to
work as a bank teller, which is tricky as jobs go because it looks
like a good job but is really a shit job all dressed up and parked
near the money. But just near, not in. We have been together
seven months, circuiting dog tracks for three. She won't marry
me because we are too new and because of her one other marriage, which got euthanized at a year, eight months.

"Can't we let the dog loose?" Tricia asks. She nudges the crate with her toe, and Tricia's Blitz sticks out his nose enough for a lick. I added that "Tricia's" part to his name just to make her happy, her name all over my life. Made him hers even though he isn't.

I shake my head, light a Marlboro, watch the water drops gather at the ends of her hair. "Best place is in the crate until race time. You build up their running until they can't stand it."

Tricia takes the cigarette from me, puffs without inhaling. She bends down and sticks her finger through the wire mesh. "Happy New Year, doggy, my Blitz," she says. Four hours now until Dick Clark lets the ball drop in New York. Out on the highway the cars are lined up, honking, the sidewalks full. We can watch from our balcony, a steady current of noisy drunks, teenagers in heat, Shriners outfitted with diapers and sashes. Tricia's Blitz whines, scratches, and Tricia pushes another pork rind through the wire. Try finding dog food on New Years' Eve in Biloxi, much less a motel room. This one was the last, I think, eighty bucks a night, and for that the paint around the door is peeling.

"Why don't you get dressed," I say. "We'll head out to one of the casinos."

She looks up at me, her brown hair drying at the edges. "With what? Think we can stuff these in the slots?" She rattles the pork-rind bag at me like Exhibit A.

"We have some money. We've placed in a few, or did you forget that?"

"Did you make us some money, hon?" She scratches the dog's ears with her fingernail, then looks up. "We have to make that last and you know it. You aren't much good at stretching things out, are you, Jack?"

I shrug. "I don't think we're doing too bad." I pick up a casino brochure off the TV and look at the photo, all those smart, happy people bathed in money and good luck, like mannequins on a hot streak, trapped in glossy folds.

"Like that goddamn car," she tells me. "A little routine maintenance and we might make Texas." The towel shifts and I look at her white thighs, the tiny purple veins that flower under her skin.

"We don't have to spend any money. Just go have a look around, not be all cooped up in here all night. It *is* New Year's."

"Now you know how the dog feels." Tricia stands and sheds her towel, her back to me. She pulls on purple panties which she won't ever let me call panties because, she says, she doesn't want anything about her to be cute, she's too old for cute. I watch her bend, watch the sway of her breast from the side, feel the twinge of knowing we will fuck, probably sometime early next year, a few hours off. I like how on this one night in the cold, a year becomes the next, and for those hours you can have something like anticipation of fucking to carry you over into another year or another decade, pretending optimism is this thing that can span a calendar instead of just being space between the links in some chain of daily screwups. And I say "fuck" because Tricia likes it, the only woman ever in my experience, because a professor she had at the community college years back hit on her every day like it was part of the syllabus and told her that the word *fuck* is a good example of onomatopoeia, like he was writing some porno grammar book and which, really, I hadn't a clue about. This word is not one I would pick up and keep. But Tricia did and when we are in bed she keeps bringing back her old prof and his old prof ideas about what happens, saying to me, *You hear that, you hear it?* And I do but don't want his idea there in the bed with us, some dictionary word to describe a thing that, in my mind, is outside any words, and I try to stamp it out by saying I can't believe she ever fell for such a lame line from an old guy, and she says that she will make no excuses for anything in her past. Only I think that's what your sum-total life *is* day by day, a renewable excuse for your past. What else? If you live well enough, if you place in a sprint stake and put money in your wallet and buy new tires and eat hot food, then all's forgiven at least till a week Tuesday. We leave a light on for Tricia's Blitz, CNN so he can hear a voice. The loneliness of dogs is not something I give much worry to.

The parking lot is all cold bluster pushing paper scraps into corners, swirling leaves into the cones of light beneath the arc lamps. Tricia slips her arm under mine, digs deep in my coat pocket for my fingers. Outside one ground-floor room are young women in thin dresses and boys in fresh haircuts and cigarette smoke and the sound of bottles knocked over. A portable CD player sits angled against the open door, and just outside, sprawled across lawn chairs and chaises, they lounge in the blast of room heat and music, an old Kinks tune kicked out fuzzy through the speaker, priming drunken bursts of song from the bunch of them. I nudge Tricia so she will see what letting go looks like, see what we ought to be like if we could get out of our own goddamn way, and she looks and smiles and roots closer to me. She sees. The whole tangle of them quit their loose-boned "Lola" long enough to whoop at us and wish us Happy etc. and ask if we have cigarettes, they are out of cigarettes, they could kill for cigarettes please oh please. On top of the dog carrier is a whole carton of Marlboros, and knowing this grooves in with their questions and wants (and those girls, those thin white arms) so nicely (*click*, and a moment is upon you) that I turn on my heel and Tricia's hand pulls from my pocket just as a question leaves her mouth, "Did you hear what they said on the news?" But I am away from her already, two at a time up the iron steps, into the room, then onto the balcony, leaning out into the wind and tossing down the sealed packs.

They gather under me, Tricia standing off a ways and cold, hugging herself, her face working out its disapproval. She does not like me giving away things, did not like it in New Hampshire, October, when Blitz placed first in the Tri-State and afterward in the bar I bought a round for everyone because it was a movie thing to do and I'd never done it, never found reason. The tab came to $164.73, a number I have kept like it's some combination to unlock what is wrong with us, but I knew then and know now that Tricia's Blitz is five, old for racing, and there are not likely any more wins left in him, and a new dog is a thousand dollars I am firmly without. So I stand there crotch against the rail and knowing that five packs of cigarettes will never add up to $164.73 and tossing them, watching them spin red and white into the raised hands and laughter below me, and for that moment I am the King of Cigarettes and the main thing I love about people and love about me loving people spins out into the wind with those shiny red packs. Tricia can't feel this, can feel only the cold that seeps into the soles of her shoes, and regards me as if I am tossing money away, which, really, I am. Tricia's Blitz watches me through his cage, sniffs me, scratches and whines. I save three packs for us, which is plenty enough till next year (three hours away?) and the kids yell up their thank-yous like trick-or-treaters, then disappear back into their light and heat and music, and close the door on Tricia and the blue arc-lamp cold and her question still hanging behind me on the stairs. She is shivering, the Gulf winds nervy and insistent.

"What?" I shout down. "What did the news say?"

She is quiet, looking up and then past me to the empty sky holding all this cold around us. Black and cold. She feels her hair with her fingertips and I can feel it too, feel how she went out with it wet and how in places it has frozen, how her warming hands unwork the ice.

"Don't be mad," I say. "Tell me." She won't answer and I take her silence, standing there like Gary Gilmore and thinking how I like it when she talks to me, how her words fill up spaces and cracks and insulate us from all the ways things turn to regret. In the long car trip down the coast I bought her a truck-stop book, *1001 Jokes for Any Occasion,* just to hear her ask me the riddles, tell the little stories of ducks and bars and nuns, to let me bounce my laughing off her words, and her laughing off mine, like we are two banks of a pond rippling back the same disturbance, the little white stone of no money and half the tracks down for winter. *Why are the Pilgrims buried in Massachusetts?* And I couldn't know, did not want to know, to take away her surprises for me. The highway rippled under us (the horn still worked then, the headliner didn't flap), and at night she kept reading jokes by the shine of the dome light when it still worked, too, and I didn't know about Pilgrims in Massachusetts, only about my hand in the groove of her thigh, my nails tracking the seam of her jeans, thin strands of her hair like moths around my face. *Because they're dead,* and the sound of laughing became the sound of moving ahead, of getting through the next town with hope intact while Tricia's Blitz slept in the rear and thoughts of a next win were still allowed.

Now she stands in the quiet, waiting for me to make things all right, to make me all right, us. Across the highway the big casino boats are lashed to the piers, docked forever, and their sound wafts across the road—locust clouds of music, deep, low *thump-thumps* of it and the static hum of too many people crowded together, these swirls of noise rising up like dust devils in the night, and inside that is me and Tricia. Here is what it's like: the man I saw on TV once making soap bubbles, bubbles inside of bubbles all angle and shimmer, and at the end he took a cigarette drag and a paper straw and filled the middle chamber with smoke. We are the smoke in this inner bubble, quiet and dark around us, noise and heat beyond that, and I know that to get to any other bubble we will have to break the one we are in.

"Tell me," I say.

"Come down."

I smile at her, watch the white bursts of her breath, and that is when I spot the raccoon, bipping around the parking lot just behind Tricia, nosing around the green Dumpster, rustling fast-food sacks. My mouth opens to tell her, but that will spook him, send him into whatever patch of woods he came from, and so I watch, quietly, his long shadow moving with him dark along the silvered pavement like something trapped under ice. We are three points on a map—me, Tricia, raccoon—allowing me to fix this moment, my brain tamping a wooden stake into right now, and seven months lie plotted around it.

"Jack, please." She lifts the collar of her coat. "Come down before I freeze to death." Her voice like thin shards of lightbulb glass scattered across a parking lot in Biloxi, and the raccoon drops its yogurt cup, regains its edginess, and slips into the dark: covert, balled, gone.

Back on the ground, I take her arm and she lets me. We walk toward Beach Boulevard. "What did the news say?" I ask.

"Awful. In Texas, near me . . . well, used to be me, these six Mexicans were crossing over illegal and they slept out between the rails and the train got them."

We stand at the curb, waiting for traffic to open and let us bolt across. Tricia seems weighted by what the news has told her, what she has felt in hearing it, and her ways of thinking open up to me. In a minute she will tell me that it does not take a lethal dose of imagination to think of waking up one last half second to a lapful of train, a faceful. Like all women, she is a pattern of caring and removal. I think of the best thing I know to say.

"Bet they were drunk and out, honey. Never saw or heard it, even a bit."

She shakes her head. "Just like you, Jack. They're Mexican so they're automatically drunk, right?" Traffic is seamless, the cars packets of debauchery and Doppler effect. Cigarettes drop through open windows and spark on the pavement. That quick, this is a fight. She pulls her hand from mine.

"That's not what I meant, Tricia. But why did they do it? Trying to stay warm? For good luck? Maybe that's the worth of superstition, thins out the dumb-asses."

Another head shake, frown. "Like you putting Blitz's silks on at the last minute, like using the same lead every time, like always holding it in your left hand, your lucky dime. Is that what's thinning us out, Jack?"

"Ten thousand riding on thirty seconds, I can do a little superstition." Traffic opens, and for a minute I feel like Moses in Detroit. We start across.

"So what did *they* have riding? Their freedom, maybe?"

Before we even make the median, she is crying over this, not something she usually tends toward. "They thought the rails protected them from snakes. Jesus." She wipes her eye with her thumb.

"Maybe they're right," I say. "Maybe it does protect them from snakes. If you have to die, at least be right." We move into the east-bound lane. Before us, the casinos drone and vibrate, five hundred polyester ladies feeding five hundred quarters to five hundred slots.

"I don't want you to be coldhearted," Tricia tells me. "And I'd rather we live and be wrong all the time."

"In that case, we're overachievers." As we near the doors, a wet heat spills out along the carpet, the odor of cheese steaks and cologne. Tricia smacks my arm to tell me she loves me still.

"You really think they were right about the snakes?" She is crying now in that way that is meant only to say how silly crying is. I guide her inside the blare and chandelier light.

"I'm positive now. Yes, ma'am. Sleeping between the tracks will by God protect you from snakes. What it won't do is protect you from trains."

She laughs, hand over her teeth. She says I am so bad, laughs, says I take the cake, laughs. The rhythm of forgiveness and more than forgiveness: gratitude that I have pulled us back from the edge of ourselves, where we teeter always, every day. I make five bucks' nickel change and let her feed a machine, her eyes still red rimmed, puffy. I tell her maybe no news might be good news for a while, that we have enough grievousness all our own without listening for more.

Give me instead, I don't say, Paul Harvey and *The Rest of the Story,* give me Ronald Reagan as a college radical, little Debbie

Reynolds and her childhood of horrific stage fright. Henry Ford, Douglas MacArthur. *That's* the news, as far as I go, the small ways we fail and succeed, all the hidden ironies that get dredged up at family reunions and funerals, making celebrities of us all, finally. And if you are God or Paul Harvey you might find pattern and meaning in it over a course of decades, enough to fill five minutes after the farm report. The rest is just sound to keep a dog company on New Year's Eve: bottle throwing in the Mideast, the stock market surging, the race for a cure, Nobel winners, bridge jumpers, the president gets caught with his finger in an intern. All of it ends up flung in some recycle bin, and even if you are God or Paul Haney it will never make a pattern and in a month or a year the market will rise/fall four hundred points and carnage will bloom across some other corner of the planet and a newly elected president will appear and we are racing still for another cure or the same. What I need (Tricia, *hear* what I'm thinking) is Paul Harvey to tell me about us, about a man and a woman and a dog. About raccoons. About a breaking-down car. I need news. I need the rest of the story.

In half an hour we are out of nickels, a band in the lounge sings Huey Lewis songs, the red carpeting sprouts cigarette burns beneath the feet of women in heels and men in tassel loafers. Potted plants. Waiters in short red jackets. Steaming buffets. Slots and megaslots. The theme of every casino is *more*. Hope, opulence, money, loss, sex, beauty. The noisy commerce of humans getting ahead. Seventy feet past us, Mississippi Sound unrolls across twenty-six miles of manmade sugary beach, the water there silty and brown from the foul mouth of the famous big river sixty miles west—muck, unswimmable even without the cold. We spear a few meatballs and cold shrimp from the long tables, make our exit still chewing, stiff-arming the icy gusts, making our way down the boulevard. The valet parking line of the Copa Casino horseshoes toward the twin towers of the building that loom bright and golden above us, a queue of white stretch limos idling, their tatters of exhaust lingering around the parking lights in a cherry mist. One of the limos draws our attention, a cartoon of a limo, ridiculous in its hugeness, its length all eased out white and shining along the curb, a hot tub bubbling where the trunk should be, tiny satellite dish affixed to the roof. The driver, an Indian man, sits on the hood thumbing *USA Today* and listening to the stereo, Al Green, through the open front door. He smokes a cigarette, lets it lip dangle, wears a black cap, black jacket, white shirt, a Notre Dame stadium blanket spread across his lap. The car looks freakish in its length. We peer in the window, cup our hands to see past the smoked glass but can't, and Tricia says you could just live here, never have to leave, and the Indian man smiles as he watches, proud of his car's ability to stun us. He hops down, moves toward us, and through my fingertips I can feel the low vibrations of the idling car, the engine up ahead somewhere in a different zip code, and I say so to Tricia to get her to laugh, like she did back when *1001 Jokes for Any Occasion* could still give up its surprises as regular as mile markers. She smiles a little, leaves her noseprint on the dark glass. The Indian wraps his Notre Dame blanket around his shoulders.

"Beautiful car," he says, as if it's ours, and I have no response but to agree, shake his hand, introduce us, wish him a Happy etc. His name is Suresh. Tricia keeps leaning to the glass, trying to see what she can't see. Suresh smiles, tells Tricia she should hire him, then he can drive her anywhere.

She shrugs at me. "Where would we go?" she says. Her nose

sports a dime of smudge from the window. "We don't have any-where."

"This car here, it has nineteen amenities," Suresh says. He begins speaking his fluent brochurese. "Luxurious leather seat-ing, full CD stereo, mirrored ceiling, romantic moon roof, dis-creet privacy divider, wet bar, TV, VCR, wall-to-wall carpet—" He halts his list. "How many is that?"

"Nine," Tricia says.

"Yes. Then there are ten more amenities. Nineteen in all."

"I wonder how hard they tried to make an even twenty," I say.

"We want to see," Tricia tells him.

"Oh, no, please. Paying only," Suresh says. He folds the front section of *USA Today*, Charlton Heston smiling, wanting every-one to buy a gun. I open my wallet, pull out ten dollars of our Jacksonville sprint stake money.

"Here," I say, pushing the money into his fist. "Now we're paying. We just want to try it out." He looks at the money, opens the door for us to sit. He tells us not to touch please anything. The leather squeaks as we slide across, the inside warm, lit a but-tery yellow, the smell of champagne and Lysol. Our faces look back at us as Suresh closes the door.

"Goddamm it, Jack," Tricia says, her arm brushing against mine. I am counting amenities: laptop computer, cell phone, microwave, tiny refrigerator.

"They should have tried harder for twenty," I say. "Twenty amenities. Sounds like a radio jingle."

Al Green runs quiet, the engine hums, Tricia breathes through her nose. "Got your ten dollars' worth yet? Just let me know when," she says. We sit not touching anything. She slips over, not touching me.

"That's just the way with amenities," I say. "Always that miss-ing one." I want her to laugh. I want this to be something we did and can remember later and it will always be that, this thing we did one night in Biloxi. *Remember that limo?* Al Green finds another song to sing, his voice all around us. Ice shifts in the champagne bucket. Tricia checks her watch, pulls her coat around her, asks if the rate is a dollar a minute. I stretch out my legs, lean back, watch us in the mirrored ceiling. My brain roots around for that missing amenity.

"Tell me a joke," I say. Tricia looks at her watch again, crosses her legs, her arms, shakes her head.

"I don't remember any jokes, Jack. Not without the book."

"Sure you do." I open the refrigerator, take out a little can of V8, pop it open, drink. "A big front porch," I say.

"What are you talking about?"

"The missing amenity. A big front porch all the way around the car, and like you said we could live in here and after we grew old we could move out to the porch and sit in rocking chairs and pass away the days together." Two swallows and I down the V8, put the empty can back in the refrigerator.

Shakes her head. "Nope. Couldn't drive around with a porch on the car. You'd be stuck. Sorry, Jack." She checks her watch. "Hour till midnight."

Since the start, she's been good at being right. Nineteen amenities, twenty, do you no good unless you can carry them with you, haul them around with you the rest of your life. What's the point of comfort if you're stuck with it? Al Green sings a sexy song about falling in love, his voice the dark smoke in the glass that surrounds us.

19 Amenities

"Okay, I remember one," Tricia says. Suresh knocks on the window.

"Better hurry." I lean back again, watch my eyes as I listen.

"An old couple about eighty or so go to this lawyer, say they've been married fifty-some years, but now they want a divorce. Lawyer says, 'Sure we can do that, we can arrange that.' Says, 'It's none of my business, but you two have been together so long, married so long, been through so much together, I have to ask why. Why divorce now?' The old lady hesitates, looks at her husband, says, 'Well, we were waiting for the children to die.'"

We sit in the absence of laughing, the tick of ice shifting in the bucket, Al Green fading toward silence. Suresh, standing where my porch would be, tries the handle. He pops the door, dome lights all around us, the wash of cold air evaporating the heat, champagne, Lysol. Evaporating the joke, the porch, the cell phone and V8 and moon roof. He shakes our hands, gives us his card. We move across the parking lot toward midnight. At the corner sits a Greyhound bus, parked on its steady hiss of air, the light inside a pale mossy green, a few scattered passengers: a man eating a sandwich, a woman in a knit hat leaning her head against the window. Tricia points—you see that?—and I do: Tricia's Blitz stretched out twenty feet along the side of the bus, metallic, silver-blue, lithe and muscled, ears pinned back in full run.

"It's beautiful," I say.

Tricia looks at me. "Well, I guess if you're into buses." She pushes back her hair. "Thing is, I'm thinking maybe of getting on one when we hit Texarkana. I mean, I don't know, Jack." I look at her, then again at the bus, try to see it as just that: a bus. Diesel burns, gears turn, it moves off toward some next thing in Texas.

I nod, waver inside. "I don't think you want to do that."

She shivers, shoves her hands inside her coat. "I don't think you know what I want. You know this whole thing is getting old, Jack."

"So we skip from too new to old, just like that. No in-between."

She thinks about this. "Well, you know, honey, about all we skipped over was indifference."

Suresh drives past us, honks, waves, his passengers hidden behind the glass. I let the wind blow, let the bus idle on gray fumes. "We can let him out if you like. Tricia's Blitz, if that's what you want."

"I would like that, sweetie. But." Her sigh is a white breath. "I'm not much of one for gestures." She checks her watch again, and I wonder if we have missed midnight, slid right past it into next year.

We make it down the iron steps and across the parking lot haul-ing the plastic crate between us, Tricia's Blitz whining inside, shifting, off balance. Tricia sweats, her face shiny in the dark, my hands stiff with cold.

"I don't see why you couldn't let him out in the room. Just walk him down to the car," Tricia says.

"He's not a pet, Tricia." I breathe, walk, stumble, shift. We pass the Dumpster, load the carrier in the back of the wagon. I open Tricia's door, fire the engine, turn the heat as high as it will go. I dig two tiny brandy bottles out of the sack and pass her one as we edge out into the bloat of traffic and slip down along the side streets until we find a high school, chains across the door handles, baseball field lit by a streetlamp. We carry the crate out to the pitcher's mound, and off in the distance I can still make out the sounds we've left behind us. Tricia stands in the batter's box and pretends to swing for the bleachers. The bases are all gone for winter. She takes off her heels so she can run, adjusts the toes of her stockings while I open the wire door, hook the long lead to Blitz's collar, unsnap his headstall, and remove his muzzle. Simple actions without words. I hook the lure (an old Davy Crockett hat, fishing weights sewn inside) to a short lead and give it to Tricia. A familiar drill: she begins running a circle around the mound and I am the point that tethers Blitz, turning with him on his lead until I spin myself into dizziness. Tricia shakes the lure—"C'mon, boy!"—then runs from me kicking up small feathers of dust as the lure hops and twists behind her, bouncing in the air, and Tricia's Blitz moves, three bounds before he's on her, Tricia laughing and calling, tugging the lure from his mouth and trailing it across the infield, circling back in a loose orbit away from me. The lead pulls me from center, and Blitz tangles himself in it; Tricia runs with the blue folds of her dress lifting around her knees, stockinged and pale, her thighs working, loose hair laced across her jawline, breath in short bursts. She slows, quits, moves toward me, Blitz behind her carrying the lure, awaiting more play.

"Can we let him off?" she says. "Just let him go this one time?"

I take the lure from Blitz, unsnap him from the long lead. He noses around his crate, peering inside. Tricia stands over home plate, swinging away at imagined fastballs, then tosses her brandy bottle in a high arc down the third base line. I hear it whistle, watch it flash in the dark, can't tell where it lands. I let go of Blitz's collar and Tricia starts toward first base trailing the lure and Blitz streams out in a gray explosion of flesh, pouncing after the lure as Tricia looks back laughing, rounding first base and Blitz bounding behind, and I think of the greyhound painted on the side of the bus, how in two days it will be like this: Tricia moving ahead, that other greyhound ten feet behind her as they move together across Texas, as if she is already there and this movement now is that, and together they make this bus that I can't see other than her motion and the painting of a perfect greyhound, one that is not five years old and too far gone for any more wins, and as they round second I try to see them this way, to fill in around them the diesel fumes and moss green windows and old ladies in hats, let my mind make a bus of the two of them, so that most of what will carry her away will not be invisible to me if I don't let it, and just as I start to see it they are rounding third and Tricia hits the gas, thighs pumping toward home, racing Blitz and laughing, swinging her arms as if there will be a close play at the plate, only there is no base, no catcher, no umpire, no one there and watching, and I wonder, who will say if she is safe or out? Who will make the call?

Mistletoe

Nelson Dillard hauled water bottles to a dusty corner of the Laundromat, one on each shoulder, setting them down hard to watch the bubbles float up bright as dimes. His mother, Myra, followed him from the delivery truck, along the rows of washers, to the vending area behind the pay phone. She moved stiffly now, the disease seeping into her leg muscles, each movement like some decision she's forced to make.

"You're sure those're distilled water, not spring water?" she asked, for the third time. She was so careful now, mindful of every detail. Nelson pointed to the label on one of the pale blue bottles: PURE MOUNTAIN VALLEY DISTILLED WATER. Myra squinted to read, then nodded, fingering the amethyst crystal she wore on a leather cord around her neck. Last month she'd given Nelson a similar necklace, along with a paperback book she said explained the ways that crystals realign the body's chakras to restore energy and vitality. She used words like "vitality" all the time now, with her new friends. The crystal and book ended up in the back of his kitchen drawer where he kept dead batteries and broken screwdrivers.

"Will it do any good to say that you ought not be working?" Nelson asked. In the corner of the Laundromat, a TV soap opera competed with a table radio playing a commercial for the Bryloff Foot Clinic. Above them, a large, gray fan slowly oscillated, trailing threads of cobwebs.

Myra waved away the question. "Do you remember Mary Alice's place, out by the fire hall?"

Nelson wiped his face on his sleeve and nodded. "Used to deliver heating oil to her. Did that house finally fall down?"

"Oh, no, she's still there." Her hand pressed his shoulder as she leaned down to whisper. "Nelson," she said, "the woman has mistletoe in her yard."

"Probably has everything else in her yard, too. That place hasn't seen hedge clippers in twenty years, I bet."

"But *mistletoe*, Nelson. Mistletoe doesn't grow around here. Too cold." He looked at her, still unable to accustom himself to the short, severe haircut she'd recently acquired, a drill sergeant's haircut. When he'd told her that she looked like a man, she said she was moving beyond gender. That's how it was now, like she'd traded in all her old words and sentences for new ones. What he didn't say was that she looked more like a cancer victim than what she really was. He could never remember the doctors' name for what she had, only that it was also called Lou Gehrig's disease. That seemed a lousy way to name something; a man plays over two thousand consecutive games and hits .340 lifetime, but it's for this everybody remembers him.

"Mistletoe, huh?" Nelson said. "I thought you quit Christmas." With a Q-tip, he cleaned the taps on the watercooler, avoiding Myra's gaze, her crew-cut hair, her wasting limbs.

"You know it's not for Christmas and it's not for kissing. Nobody is about to kiss some dying old bitch."

Nelson winced, tossed the dirty Q-tip in the trash. Beside them, two women smoked cigarettes and argued about the best way to stuff comforters and pillows into one of the big Dexter double-load machines.

"What then?" Nelson said, not really wanting to hear the answer.

"Well, according to the book, the berries are highly toxic and produce a peaceful death. The Druids worshipped mistletoe, Nelson. They thought it was sacred. Navajos made amulets from it."

He opened the clean tap and let the water flow out, big bubbles gurgling up through the tank as he wiped his hands on his thighs. "Navajos and Druids." He shook his head. "That goddamn book."

"That's right," she said, her voice uncertain. "That goddamn book that's going to see me through all this."

"See you out of it, you mean."

"That, too. Are you coming to my party? This is the eighth time I've asked you."

"And the eighth time I've said no. Getting the message?" He stood, taller than her by a foot, his own close-clipped hair brushing the yellowed cardboard sign dangling by its string from the ceiling fan. He knew without looking that it advertised All-Brite Powder. It had been hung there thirty years prior, when Nelson was nineteen and his mother and father had bought the Laundromat, and within a week the salesmen came swarming around with their brochures for washing machines and vending machines and soap powders, with their posters and free samples and business cards. All that excitement and new money, everything bright and shiny and clean, and Sunday evenings were fried chicken and *The Ed Sullivan Show* and TV trays in the den, Nelson living in the apartment his father had fashioned above the garage, where two years later he lived with Jennifer after their marriage at the Baptist church. Now Jennifer had moved off into a new marriage and real-estate sales, his father had been dead eight years, and his mother had slowly drifted away from everything Nelson thought of as normal, as though his father's existence had been a paperweight, anchoring Myra to a regular life. He thumped the All-Brite sign with his finger. "Don't ask me again," he said.

Myra lifted her hands and watched herself flex them, as if they were kitchen gadgets she had not yet figured out how to work. He tried to imagine how it must feel to her, the disease filling her bones, emptying her muscles.

"I won't ask, Nelson. Thank Goddess that Roxie will be there. You'll hate yourself someday."

"Do you have to say that?"

"It's true, you will. I know a few things after sixty-eight years."

"I mean the 'Goddess' part. I hate that."

She fingered the fringes of her choppy hair. "Like that's the worst of my problems, what you hate." He couldn't face another gathering, what she insisted this time on calling her "bon voyage party." The plan was to say good-bye to everyone, give away her things to friends, celebrate her life with alcohol and snack mix, and then within a week or two dig out of that book some quick and easy way to kill herself, as in earlier years she might have found a recipe for pound cake. At the first party she announced her decision to "embrace her death" rather than fight it, and all her friends applauded and kissed her. She introduced one of them as a "midwife," whose job it was to assist Myra as she delivered herself from this world and into the next. He'd just stood there, hearing them speak this way.

She sighed. "If you won't come to the party, at least promise to get the mistletoe for me. Be some use to me. And it's not like I'm asking you to be there when the time comes." Myra reached in her smock and automatically brought out a handful of quarters for the little boy who approached them with a dollar wadded in his fingertips. He was a skinny, pinkish boy who looked to be about seven years old, wire-rimmed glasses low on his nose. His other hand held a baby doll with a missing arm and matted blond hair. His grandmother helped out at the Laundromat three afternoons a week.

"*Get* the mistletoe? Why don't I just *get* my shotgun?" Nelson's face heated up.

"Lower your voice, please," Myra said, nodding at the boy, who stood with his pale mouth slightly open, eyes wide behind the quarter-size lenses.

Nelson looked at him. "No, it's okay, I'm not going to be shooting anybody." He felt his pockets for something to give the boy. "Tell me your name again, son."

"Earl." He chewed his lower lip. "My daddy's name, too."

"Earl is our little helper-outer," Myra said.

Nelson found a key-chain bottle opener with RUSTY'S LIQUORS printed on the side. He gave it to Earl, who looped the chain over the head of his doll for a necklace. He shook the doll to make the necklace swing back and forth, then ran off toward his grandmother behind the front counter. Nelson looked at Myra. Her blouse, her pants, shoes, all her clothes had been altered to fasten with Velcro.

"The party is Saturday night, in case you change your mind. I'd like you to change your mind."

He shook his head, drew a deep breath, the air around them heavy with the smell of scorched sheets. "I'll see you later," he said.

Nelson had deliveries to make by Friday: three tanks of helium for Pizza Palace, liquid hydrogen for the hospital, water bottles to the office park, concrete mix to some guy building a garage. Roxie was at home, fixing lunch. He sat in the truck, chewing one of the ginseng toothpicks Myra had given him to help him quit smoking. For all of his adult life he'd been delivering something to somebody. When Roxie was studying for her degree, she told him that a writer named Ralph Waldo Emerson once said, "Make yourself necessary to somebody." She told Nelson that's what he did, with the delivery business he'd had since he was eighteen and bought his first pickup. Nelson liked the way Roxie could make what he did sound important and indispensable. He'd written the quote on a notecard and taped it to the visor next to his roadmap holder and looked at it now as he cranked the engine, pulling out down Taylor Avenue toward Mary Alice's place.

The house stood in the middle of fast-food restaurants, gas stations, convenience stores. A small wire fence guarded the weedy yard, the broken walkway lined with cement blocks and headless, unpainted lawn ornaments of squirrels and deer. The brown asbestos shingles that covered the house were wrapped in a layer of kudzu, the tendrils of the vines stretching up the chimney and along the far wall. The house looked sunken, as if it had drawn back from all the commerce that surrounded it. Two Chihuahuas sat panting in a ring of dirt where the grass had worn away, the ring marking the length of the chains that tethered them to the dog house. Above them, dense as a thundercloud, was an oak tree, and in the middle and top branches were the darker green patches of mistletoe spotted with white berries. He tried to imagine what it would feel like, swallowing the berries, the slow wait as their poison wound through the bloodstream, snapping out nerves like light switches, shutting down the lungs, the heart. She'd found out about it from the suicide book she'd gotten from the Hemlock Society. The book had some lavish title meant to make killing yourself sound reasoned and noble. At her first party Myra told a variation of the old funeral parlor joke, saying that the Hemlock Society must not be a very good club, seeing how everyone was dying to get out. Her friends laughed like she'd said something cute.

Why was it nothing mattered to anyone anymore?

Without much thought, Nelson stepped up to Mary Alice's rotted porch and knocked. Tacked to the doorframe was a recent notice to condemn. They were booting her out, finally, squeezing in another car wash or Taco Bell. Nelson knocked again. From inside came the faint sounds of shuffling and things knocked over. She was a mean old woman, he knew from the years delivering heating oil to her house. He'd ask about the mistletoe, she'd chase him from the yard, and that would end it; he would have his excuse for Myra. The latch on the door sounded. Through the window Mary Alice looked like a shrunken version of his memory of her, her hair fully white now and thinning, her apple-doll mouth puckered brown, her eyes a whitish blue.

She swung the door open, looked at him through the dirty screen. "You here to see to those moles?"

"Ma'am? No, I just wanted to ask you something."

"My daughter-in-law hates me," Mary Alice said, her voice trailing to a mumble. As he leaned to hear her, Nelson noticed her smell, like creosote and attic trunks, and her feet, covered in men's wingtip shoes bound with twine.

"I bet she doesn't hate you," Nelson said. He didn't know what else to say. "Do you know your oak tree is full of mistletoe?" Beneath thinning hair, her scalp was bright pink and spotted.

"Just another parasite. That's all there is anymore. Them moles, my daughter-in-law. The whole list." A can of tuna fish sat open on the hall table behind her.

"Looks like the county is on that list, too," Nelson said. She squinted at him. "They mean to condemn your place and take it, ma'am."

She made a grunting noise. "Like to see that happen. See them try that again."

Nelson shrugged. "It's not really a matter of trying. They just go on ahead." He thumped the notice stapled to her doorframe. "What I wondered was if I could take some of that mistletoe out of your tree before they take it down with a bulldozer."

She frowned at him. "You get rid of those moles, you can take anything you want, except my dogs. They caught my asthma from me, you know."

"Ma'am, I'm not really here about your moles . . ." He

stopped, not wanting to get into the whole thing again. She looked at him, blinking. He told her he would do what he could. As he climbed into his truck, he took another look at the clumps of mistletoe high in the tree. She pushed open the screen door to shout after him.

"Don't you put down any poison," she said, her thin voice a wire stretched across the yard. "You'll kill my dogs if you do."

"I've said it before, I think you should go," Roxie said. She sat at her small desk, hands busy with changing the ribbon in her typewriter. Since her degree in English from the state college, she'd had a job writing captions for the Walter Drake household gift catalogue. So far this afternoon she had finished up descriptions of an electric callus remover and a bathtub safety seat. She was working on a sheepskin recliner cover when the ribbon went out.

Nelson nodded, rubbed his face, finished his fried chicken. "She wants me to bring poison to the party."

"Poison?" Roxie looked at him.

"Yeah, you know, the way other people bring beer."

"What poison?"

Her told her about Myra's request, about Mary Alice and the moles. She leaned her head on her typewriter, looking at him. "What are you going to do?"

Nelson sighed. "I'm not going to kill my mother, Rox. Let her call what's-his-name, that Dr. Death guy. Did he retire or something?"

"In a way, though, it's her last wish. It's the last thing you could do for her. Giving her an easy death isn't such a bad thing, Nelson."

"Don't even start that."

She pulled her long braid across her shoulder, fingering it. "You talked to her doctors. You know what's in store. It takes a long time, Nelson, and someday she won't be able to chew. Won't be able to talk or move or swallow."

Nelson held a bite of fried chicken in his mouth until the saliva pooling around it threatened to choke him.

"At least go to her party," Roxie said.

"Her party." Nelson shook his head. "You weren't there for the first one. She went around telling everybody she'd rather have Babe Ruth's disease, so she'd only have to deal with getting fat and drinking a lot."

Roxie smiled.

"That's not funny," Nelson said.

"Well, it isn't and it is," she said. "You can't stop her from dying, honey."

That was the part he knew, that she would die, and that all she wanted with the mistletoe berries or the Hemlock Society or the books she read was a way to speed things up and make it happen sooner. But it was just wrong, somehow. He saw this early on in his business, when he first had the truck, how he tried to impress everybody by making deliveries early, but only messed everybody up. They couldn't put the carpet down until the floors were finished, or had no place to stack bottles until the steel shelving was up. He learned to wait until it was time. Maybe tragedy had its own time, its own schedule, and to hurry it up would do nothing but compound it. Maybe something wasn't ready, maybe Myra herself, or some eleventh-hour cure some doctor might happen upon, or maybe . . . something. As for God, heaven, souls . . . it was hard for him to think of it, and

Myra had given all that up when Nelson's father died, as though she had worn out her faith or just let it go. He looked at Roxie, her hands striped with ink from the new ribbon.

"I don't know about any of this," he said.

"You don't have to decide right away," she said. She wiped her hands on crumbled-up paper and turned back to her work. She typed, then stopped. "How does this sound? 'Relax in durable comfort.'"

Nelson shook his head. "Can't imagine that there is such a thing."

That night, his hand resting on the curve of Roxie's hip as she slept beside him, Nelson slipped into half dreams of walking, he and his father, in the bone cold of winter that came to the Ozarks after an eye blink of autumn. Early December, his father crunching through drifts in stiff rubber boots to a field behind Singleton's Tire Shop, where a forty-foot oak threw gnarled shadows across Davidson Street. His father smoked a cheap, sweet-smelling cigar and carried a shotgun crooked under his arm. Other men gathered there, smoking, drinking from Thermoses or Dixie cups. One at a time they loaded paper shells into their guns, took sloppy aim, and fired into the upper branches of the oak. Early morning or early evening, he couldn't remember, the sky marbled, sparse cars slipping on the road behind them. With no word the next took aim at the tree and fired, then came the nudge of his daddy's thumb against his shoulder and Nelson ran to gather the clumps of mistletoe that had fallen, separating them from the broken branches cut through white and brittle, flecked with shotgun pellets. He stuffed the green

leaves and white berries into grocery sacks, and at home his
mother and the other men's wives would wire together small
bundles tied off with red ribbon and slipped into plastic sandwich bags. A dollar each, sold in the grocery store and the card
store, or by Nelson door to door. They did this every Christmas.

Once, while he was gathering bundles, one of the men raised
his gun and fired without waiting for Nelson to retreat back to
their group. All the other men shouted, some of them laughing,
the pellets falling like finger thumps along the top of Nelson's
skull. He pressed back against the tree trunk and watched his
father grab the gun barrel and twist it upward. Above him a few
stray pellets tapped like rain through the tree branches, and as
Nelson listened he felt only a kind of assurance. He was nine
years old. He would grow up. He would be an adult with a life
as full and troubled and real as his father's or his father's friends.
He would have a wife someday, kids (he'd been wrong on that
part), his life would continue on and was not about to be ended
by some shotgun accident notable mainly for its stupidity. It
wouldn't happen that way. Now, at forty-nine, lying in the dark
beside Roxie, what did his life have left in the way of assur-
ances? A job that never changed, a woman who needed him
only in ways. None like he had at nine, knowing that no threat
could touch him, and none like those he carried into adulthood,
the belief that someone, somewhere, would find you and love
you completely, that your life would turn out to be something
rather than just things. He lifted his fingers from under the
sheet and toward the darkened ceiling. What thing might be
left to hold in your hands? What might be left to know?

.　.　.

The next morning, while he picked up a load of peat moss at Scott Seed, he asked the man working there about the best way to get rid of moles.

"Mothballs," the man said. He rubbed a cigarette out on the bottom of his shoe. "Shove them down the tunnels and wait."

Nelson shook his head. "No poison. Dogs might dig it up."

The man scratched his head, looked at his cold cigarette butt. "Flooding them out can work, kind of a Noah's Ark trick. Or this." He walked over to a display and lifted a pair of bright plastic daisies, pinwheels made to spin on wire posts. "You stick 'em in the ground and the wind makes them turn. Supposed to drive the moles crazy. Doesn't look to me like it'd work worth a damn. Some things are just hard to kill."

Nelson nodded, picked up one of the daisies, and turned it with his finger. The salesman left for a minute then returned, handed Nelson a plastic-wrapped package.

"Here's the latest thing," he said. "Snake." He opened the package and unfurled a six-foot section of vinyl, one end with a plastic valve like a beach ball. The snake was brown and gold, patterned to look like a copperhead. The salesman blew, red-faced, inflating the snake to a puffy **S**.

He closed the valve and handed the snake to Nelson. "If we can't drive them crazy, we'll give them heart attacks."

Nelson turned it over in his hands. It smelled like a shower curtain. "This works?"

"I don't know if it works. Snakes are natural enemies of most rodents, most birds. Couldn't hurt, I figure."

Nelson left the store with half a dozen of the daisies and the snake, the air let out of it. He drove to Mary Alice's house, placed the windmills around the weedy yard, and with loops of baling

wire from the truck anchored the snake to the packed dirt
beneath the tree. With every other step the earth caved in and
he fell ankle deep into the mole tunnels. He finished his work,
looked at the strange sproutings around him, the bright, over-
large flowers motionless without a breeze. The Chihuahuas
edged up to the snake and sniffed it, ran in a circle then sniffed
some more.

"You mutts better watch out," he said to them. "You're dealing with a natural enemy." He edged under the oak and looked
up at the dark patches of mistletoe, the tiny white berries. His
hand smoothed along the trunk and slid up the first branch. He
gripped it, pulled until his arms began to shake. It had been too
long since he'd tried to climb trees. But he could get it. One way
or another he could bring the mistletoe down and hold it in his
hands and carry with him all its poison and promise of quick
death. A parasite, feeding off the fear of a disease named for
some long-dead baseball player. The whole thing was strange,
this chain of connections that wound somehow around and
through Nelson. He looked up, tossed a rock at the mistletoe,
watched it bounce in the parking lot of the car wash next door.
What he would give Myra for her party, he decided, was the
refusal to help her die. To hold in his hands the leaves and white
berries and to *not* give it, make a show of not giving it, of not
poisoning her, of not letting her take herself from this life.

He stepped onto the porch and knocked on the door.

"Ma'am?" he shouted through the door. "I think I took care
of your moles." He bent to peer inside. "Mary Alice?" He saw
only her shadow moving along the kitchen wall, sliding up it
dark and liquid, heard the squeak and bang of kitchen cabinets,
the rasp of her shuffle, the thin clang of stove pans.

. . .

After lunch of grilled cheese sandwiches and descriptions of a vacuum extender and a full-page magnifier, he drove to the Laundromat. There he found Myra sitting in a plastic chair next to a magazine rack and crying. Around her scattered everywhere on the floor were dimes and quarters, change for the machines which she'd spilled from her apron pocket. Nelson bent to help pick them up, along with a woman in a sweatsuit and gold bracelets, and Earl, the small boy with the doll. Earl kept filling his hands, dumping the money back into Myra's apron.

"Look at these," Myra said to Nelson, flexing her hands. "Just useless." They quivered as she tried to bunch them into fists. Her short hair shifted color in the light. Nelson found the last of her dimes and gave it to Earl. The Laundromat was decorated for tomorrow's party, which she had decided to have there instead of her tiny apartment. This had always been more her home anyway, she said. The walls rippled with hanging strips of crepe paper, the ceiling fans with plastic champagne glasses suspended from fish line. Along the back wall a large banner read BON VOYAGE in bright red letters surrounded by drawings of confetti and noise makers. Two of Myra's friends stood on step ladders, hanging a poster: *25 REASONS TO EMBRACE YOUR JOY OF BLESSING*. They smiled at each other as they worked, spoke in quiet voices under the hum of washers and dryers. Reason six was, "The Earth Is Your Path to Expanding Illumination."

Myra kept quietly crying, hands held in her lap as if someone had dropped them there. Nelson knelt and took her hands in his. Earl stood beside her chair, patting her on the shoulder.

"Do you see now that you have to let the doctors help you?" Nelson said. "They have medicine to make you feel better. The interferon treatment. They said they can stabilize the disease."

She shook her head. "Just listen to yourself, Nelson. *Stabilize* my disease. My dis-ease. No thanks." She stood, wiped her face, smoothed her slacks out along her thighs, jingled the coins in her apron. She looked around at the decorations. "Are you coming to my party tomorrow?"

"Yes, I am."

Her face, suddenly alive, turned up at him. "And my mistletoe?"

"Are you really going to use that, when the time comes?" This was their phrase, the way they had of talking around it. At first, Myra had always referred to it as her "rebirth," and made jokes about becoming a born again, or about coming back as one of her own double-load machines. Finally Nelson had asked her to stop making jokes.

"My midwife thinks it's a good choice. We're still negotiating this. I don't want any method that anyone is going to have to clean up."

"For godsakes, Myra." Nelson shook his head, looked away from her. The women were hanging a big photo of a sunset beside the 25 Reasons poster. Reason seventeen was, "You Are the Master of Your Own Ascension."

"Get me the mistletoe, Nelson, and maybe I won't strike you from the will." She put her hand on the back of his wrist, tiny tremors carried inside her fingers. "It would mean something to me. I don't plan on falling into a lot of weepy sentiment about this. I don't have the energy, or the time. But you should know, it will mean something to me."

"You want my blessing. You want me to just let you take yourself out when you might have years left. When you could be stabilized." Behind the Coke machine was a small door to the basement incinerator, long unused. He saw himself opening the door, tossing the clump of mistletoe down the dark chute as the women stood watching him, silent, champagne glasses in their hands. He felt for a moment the weight of meanness in what he would do, along with the twin weight of seriousness. Let them know that death is not a party, that loss is not an occasion for fun, that the heft of life could not be contained in some goddamn feel-good poster. He was doing them all a favor.

"Okay," he said. "I will get it. If Earl here is any good at climbing trees."

Earl looked up at him, the pink doll in his hand, the Rusty's Liquors key chain still looped around its neck. "I can," he said. "Just let me up that tree."

"Let's go, then," Nelson said. He touched Earl on the shoulder.

"Nelson, it's getting dark out, and he needs to ask his grandma anyway." Brenda was at the front of the store, working the counter.

"Well, ask her, then, and we'll go first thing tomorrow, soon as you open up here." Earl nodded and ran off to ask. Myra let a handful of coins rain through her fingers and into her pocket, a nervous habit she'd never let go, a souvenir of her old life.

"Party starts at one," she said. "And you wear something bright. You show up wearing some old dark suit and a black armband, I won't let you in the door."

"I'll wear a Hawaiian shirt, Myra. I'll wave bye-bye if it makes you happy."

. . .

By early the next morning, Myra had filled the sorting table at the back of the store with her own old stuff, boxed and gift wrapped. Roxie was there already, too, had left that morning wearing a bright sundress. She'd brought with her salsa and guacamole, and was busying herself in the back, setting out paper cups and napkins. Nelson pulled Earl away from the smells of champagne punch and cake, toward his truck in the parking lot. Right away, Earl began asking every question he could think of, wondering if he could try driving, if the truck could do a wheelie, what it was that Nelson had stacked in the back of the truck.

"I know something you'd like," Nelson said. He jumped up into the bed and patted his hand against one of the tanks of helium he had to deliver to Pizza Palace, the top of the tank painted to look like a clown. Nelson turned the nozzle and let the cold gas blow inside his mouth, sucking down mouthfuls of it.

"Ready to climb that tree, Earl?" Nelson said in a high, Donald Duck voice. Earl only looked at Nelson and blinked.

"How did you do that?" He looked a little bit afraid.

"Helium," Nelson said, his voice normal again. "It's an old trick."

In the cab of the truck, Earl opened the glove compartment and pushed his doll inside, dug around under the seats for bottle caps and spare change, and would not stop asking questions. Soon enough they pulled up in front of Mary Alice's house and Nelson set the brake.

"This is the place, and that's the tree," Nelson said. "Think you can handle it?"

"I climbed bigger trees when I was a baby." He pulled his doll from the glove box and stuffed it into his jeans pocket. Nelson headed to the front door to tell Mary Alice that they would be climbing her tree. Across the yard his boots broke through into the tunnels, the weeds caving with each step. Stapled to the door was a second notice to condemn, this one bigger, the names and dates all filled in with ink. He knocked, heard her movements inside, cupped his hands against the glass. He saw nothing but stacks of newspapers, a box of grocery store fire logs. Behind him, he heard crying.

Earl had climbed up about twelve feet and gotten stuck in the lower branches of the oak, afraid to move up or jump down. Nelson walked toward him, stepping into holes, turning his ankles. The Chihuahuas lay sleeping at the base of the tree. Beside them was the vinyl snake, flattened and full of tiny bite marks. It was late morning, the sun high above them, the shadow of the tree narrow and dark green. The plastic daisies slowly turned in a faint breeze. The party would start in an hour, and he imagined them already opening their presents, smiling and kissing Myra as she gave away little bits of her life. Earl sat on one branch, clutching the other above him, his doll on the ground, in the roots of the tree where he had dropped it. The first cluster of mistletoe was at least forty feet above him, impossible to reach.

"Come down out of there," Nelson said.

"I can't," he said. His glasses had slid down his nose, and he let go just long enough to push them up.

"Sure, and I'll catch you. We'll see about your doll."

Nelson heard the screen door squeak and turned to see Mary Alice step onto the porch. She grabbed the bottom of the condemn notice and pulled on it, leaning back and shaking until the cardboard tore loose of the staples. She wore a man's suitcoat over her dress, and held the condemn notice to her chest like a girl carrying schoolbooks.

"You get that boy out of that tree," she yelled, her voice watery. "Before he breaks his neck."

"I think she means it, son," Nelson said.

Without another word, Earl turned and slid backward out of the tree, and Nelson caught him under the arms. Nelson told him to wait in the truck, then walked over to Mary Alice.

"Did you come about those moles?" she asked him. "My daughter-in-law hates me."

For godsake, Nelson thought, and closed his eyes a moment. This is what it came to. You live your life the best way you can, and this is what's waiting for you at the end.

"Ma'am? I have to tell you, I think those moles are here to stay."

Her mouth worked noiselessly, as if searching out words. Nelson turned to leave. He didn't know what else to do. As he moved across the yard, the dirt gave way again and he stumbled, tore his pants and his knee on the rocky ground.

"God*dammi*t," he said. He walked around the back of the house, found a pile of rusting tools next to the water meter, and dug through until he found a shovel with a broken handle. He carried it to the front, jabbed the blade in the ground, and levered his weight against it, spading up the tunnels. His hands shook as he dug, his breath escaping in wet bursts. Again and again, he stuck the shovel into the dirt until he unearthed a nest of moles, white and shrunken, writhing on the blade. He stopped, his breath ragged. They were no larger than his thumb, hairless, their eyes tiny slits. He watched them move, blind and so narrowly alive. He dumped them onto the hard ground, put the blade against the first one, and severed it in two. He killed another, then another, as a tiny pool spread across the dirt.

"You gonna mash 'em all?" Earl spoke, standing suddenly in front of Nelson, watching him. Nelson leaned on the shovel and looked across the wide expanse of yard, the network of tunnels. There would be hundreds of them, thousands, more. Tiny and white and blind, filling the ground under Mary Alice's house. He looked around. Mary Alice ignored them now, and sat on the porch bench tearing strips off the condemn notice and stuffing them into her ruined shoes.

He let his breathing settle down. "I guess I'm not," he said. He lifted the remaining moles, watched as they tried to burrow into the blade, then turned his wrist so that they fell back into the hole. Just as he began scooping dirt back into the hole, Earl dropped his doll down the tunnel.

Nelson stopped shoveling. "What are you doing?"

Earl shrugged. "He got killed when he fell out of that tree."

"Baloney. I'll fix it up for you, good as new."

Earl shrugged. "It don't matter."

"Are you sure?" Earl nodded and Nelson spaded up a blade-ful of soil, buried the doll with the moles. He packed the dirt with his foot, replaced the shovel, and on the way back to the truck retrieved the ruined snake.

"What's that?" Earl said.

"A blow-up snake," Nelson said. "It's supposed to scare things away, but I don't think it's working."

Earl shook his head and waited for Nelson to explain. Nelson found a roll of duct tape on the floorboard of the truck and patched the vinyl, the copperhead spotted with squares of gray. After three hard puffs left him breathless, Nelson climbed into the bed of the truck and turned the nozzle on the Pizza Palace helium tank. He opened the valve of the snake and let it swallow the hiss of gas, slowly filling along its length. When it was tight he closed off the nozzle, and bounced the copperhead like a ball on the air.

"Got one more job for you," Nelson said.

"What?" Earl reached and touched the snake.

"See how long you can keep your eye on it, not let it out of your sight." Nelson pulled away his hand and the snake rose, twisting as it ascended, shifting on thermals and faint breezes. It pulled away over the tree and the house, over the fast-food places and car lots, over Mary Alice filling her shoes with cardboard, over the Laundromat five miles away where the party was starting, Myra laughing and laughing with all her old friends. Earl stood cupping his hands to his eyes, serious and intent. The snake lifted higher still, rose to a faint ink squiggle against the sky, and then, in the time it takes one moment to become the next, disappeared.

Those Imagined Lives

Why does the universe go to all the bother of existing?

—Stephen Hawking

Across three days of driving from West Virginia to northern Utah, Weimer had turned the word over in his head, fingering its crevices and edges: *Affair.* This, after the stilled and empty days following the events that the word represented, after the talks and affirmations, the reprehensions and admittances, and after Shawna had broken seven of the ceramic serving platters she made and sold through gift shops in Berkeley Springs. Weimer would have favored more noise and anguish, would have preferred the platters smashed against the wall to the way Shawna had lifted them one at a time, snapped them over her knee, and quietly stacked the ruined pieces on the kitchen table.

Somewhere near I-80 in Nebraska, he'd allowed himself a last thought of Leah Bowen (her bulky hair, that tiny gap in her teeth) and resolved to turn his thoughts back to his good and faithful Shawna, his undeserved Shawna, back to that sad stripe of clay down the thigh of her jeans. In the same moment, he decided that he didn't like the word, after all. *Affair*. He said it out loud to the car, to the fast-food wrappers on the floorboard, to the announcer on the radio. The word made him think of the movies his younger colleagues preferred, those old black-and-whites they found in the classics section of the video store. *Affair*. A Cary Grant word, or William Holden. Martinis and cigarettes and cobbled streets in Paris. It romanticized what had been nothing more than three months of occasional, almost rote afternoons in the apartment of the young woman who ran the AmeriCorps program at the high school where Weimer taught physics and calculus, a woman who e-mailed him because the phone took too much time, who attended weekend raves over in Morgantown ("West Virginia has *raves?*" Weimer had said, when she told him). After he finally called things off, she shrugged, said, "Yeah, all right," and offered him a Dos Equis.

Entanglement, he'd tried for a while, when he was only ten miles from Lisk's house in the middle of God-knows-where, and after he'd left phone messages for Shawna, talking to his own machine in response to his own invitation to do so, and after his Frank Sinatra CD had gotten stuck in the player, then the paperclip he used to try to retrieve the CD, then the Bic cap he used to try to retrieve *that*.

Entanglement wasn't it, either.

"Warm bodies," Lisk said, an hour later. "That's the phrase you're looking for. See, you want to objectify the whole thing, when all we're really talking is a few lies from your mouth and an exchange of fluids, right? You fucked and you fucked up.

They sound alike, bro, but the concepts are way different." He thought for a second. "What do they call that?"

An old corduroy couch occupied most of the small deck on the front of Lisk's modular house where they sat drinking tequila sunrises, staring off at the flat, black loaf of I-80 cooking in the August heat. A corner of the deck was taken up by a decent-size Dob telescope, which belonged to Lisk's girlfriend, Maysoon, an astrophysicist, the real thing, who'd moved to the desert to continue her work on dark matter, doing large-scale velocity measurements at the university while working on a digitized model of the universe. Her work brought her here, as Lisk's troubles with the feds had brought him; no one, Lisk said, ended up here by accident.

"What do they call what?" Weimer said. He drank and watched Lisk, who was watching the ice in his drink. They had not seen each other in five years, though they'd stayed in touch with late-night phone calls and their correspondence games of chess.

"You know, words that pull double duty like that," Lisk said.

"Homonyms," Maysoon said from behind them. She brought them each a thick hamburger lush with ketchup and onion, plus french fries heaped on a paper plate. She bit deeply into her burger, her tiny frameless glasses moving as she chewed, the octagonal lenses obscuring her dark-eyed intelligence. Weimer had always thought her oddly attractive with her choppy hair, her crooked teeth, her smoothed and angled face of vaguely Asian origins. She was five months pregnant and wearing a black sports bra, the smooth, brown camber of her bare stomach beautiful and insistent. Weimer wished then that Shawna hadn't draped herself with those maternity tents when she'd been pregnant, or that he'd asked to see the progression of her own curving flesh.

"Hey, bro," Lisk said, "I want to show you something."

Weimer chewed. "Is it legal?" Lisk had started his arsenal of guns at fourteen and had been growing it ever since, along with all his trouble and paranoia.

Lisk shrugged. "Out here, no one cares."

"You know, there are translanguage homonyms," Maysoon said. Her burger was gone already, like a magic trick.

"What do you mean?" Weimer asked.

"My mentor, Dr. Van der Shaar, never says a word, right? He gets a little drunk at a faculty party and starts telling us this stuff. You know what this means, 'fry'?" She held up one of her soggy french fries.

"Not a clue," Weimer said.

"The car," Lisk said, ignoring her, too caught up in his own plans. "Did you see it out back?"

"In Dutch," Maysoon said, "'fry' sounds exactly like 'vrij,' which means 'I make love'." She smiled at Weimer. For a few seconds, he tried to pretend she was flirting. "Ask me what 'Spain' means," she said.

"It means 'Weimer is still pissing his life away,'" Lisk said.

"Thanks for the vote of confidence," Weimer said.

Lisk grabbed his forearm. "You didn't answer me. The Impala, did you see it?"

"I did. It's a beauty. Especially if you're fifty-five years old and it's 1973."

Lisk's wet mouth hung open. "Hey, I paid a good eighty bucks for that car. Eighty bucks that's supposed to go to Uncle Sam."

"Your good, old Uncle Sam," Weimer said. "Have you two patched things up?"

"He tends to hold a grudge," Lisk said.

" 'Spain' means 'nipple,' " Maysoon told them. She frowned this time. "Language is like . . . *rubber*. I don't see how the linguistics people stand it." She held her hands under her belly, like a five-year-old holding a bowling ball. Then she looked up at the sky. She was always, in all the years he'd known her, looking up at the sky without the benefit of her Dob or light collectors, with only her naked eye, as if something might happen up there and she would miss the whole thing. She leaned back to look, her throat long and smooth. How much time had passed since Weimer had taken notice of Shawna's throat, of those little wisps of hair along her neck, the freckles on her upper chest, all the things that had drawn him into what he assumed to be, having no other words for it, love with her? The thin whisper of guilt in his ear, asking real questions instead of the rhetorical kind. And so he guessed *a long time* as his answer, thinking that maybe thirteen years had exponentially dulled his ability to see her. Then again, his brain argued back, when he *did* see her, it was always just that. Just her.

He'd thought of all these things during the drive up, when he wasn't thinking of ways to name his betrayal (*Betrayal?*), thought of his wife and the woman she'd made herself into over their space of life together, and he tried to see her not as his wife but as some separate being, an entity apart from him, and it shocked him, right outside Provo, how easy it was to do this. Not because of his apartness from her, but because of hers from him. His misplacing (*Misplacement?*) of affection had been this dumb, blind, weighted thing, a wrecking ball swung at midnight through the mortared center of their lives, but instead of demolishing her it had simply broken her free. Freedom from or freedom to, he wondered, recalling some undergraduate course in ethics. But of course it was freedom from, *always* freedom from; that's why she'd been so calm when she destroyed her ceramics. And why the whole thing scared him down to his bone marrow. What—the question insisted itself, the sum of all his worry—had he done?

"So what's with the car?" he asked Lisk.

"Schemes, plots." Lisk drank. Maysoon slid her chair next to his and took his hand. "Game plans and contrivances."

Weimer nodded and looked out over the flattened landscape, the long hyphen of highway visible to them, the puncture of sunlight in the sky. Their backyard, Lisk had said, was thirty thousand acres of salt flats. The air here smelled vaguely of burned laundry, and try as he might, he could see no potential for anything resembling a game plan or contrivance in all this emptiness. But he didn't say this, knowing that Lisk would shake his head and accuse Weimer of yet another failure of imagination. Their last year at Hopkins, Lisk had made plans to go do service observations for Goddard, while Weimer had quietly taken a teaching job at the Catholic high school. Since then, whenever Weimer complained about his job, Lisk would shake his head as if some tragedy had occurred, and say to Weimer, always, the same thing: "Welt, *mi amigo*, don't blame the macrocosm if you opt for triviality."

They sat drinking and watching the slow arc of the sun toward evening. At one point Weimer realized that he'd been here five hours and had not yet been inside the house. Three times he and Lisk had ambled out into the sagebrush to pee, and once Lisk had pulled a pistol from his belt and fired it off into the empty desert. Weimer looked at him, only half-surprised. These were old habits. Lisk himself had of course gotten older and thicker. His hair, which he still wore in a thin, braided ponytail, had mostly disappeared on top, as if it had escaped down his back with bedsheets knotted together. And he still wore the black-framed army-issue glasses, their clunkiness lending him the look of some late-sixties underground radical group member. This was, Weimer had always supposed, his reason for wearing them.

And then it was nothing but moonlight and yellow porch light, the two of them drunk, Maysoon inside napping on the couch. Lisk took him out back, opened the trunk of the Impala, and pulled out cans of spray paint, the little balls rattling inside as he shook them. He'd always been a man with a relationship to car trunks. In high school he'd rigged the trunk of his Nova with nitrous oxide to kick the drag racing butts of all the rednecks on Stratford Road, and in college would travel home for the weekend and bring back a trunkload of moonshine in plastic milk jugs. For six months, the spare tire well of his Honda hid the plans and prototype for a submachine gun he'd invented, a device which, he liked to brag, weighed only four pounds and fired thirty-five hundred rounds per minute. In a tantrum over being turned down by the U.S. Army, he had sold his designs to the Saudis for a suitcase full of money. In the end he hadn't broken any laws, only roughed up a few, but the men with the shiny suits and hair oil spent six months keeping him under surveillance, and every year for the past eight his taxes have been audited. There is nothing like persecution, he said once, to fuel your paranoia.

In the milky dark, they painted the Impala with wide loops of Day-Glo orange and green. The better, Lisk said, to see it. Weimer had the same motivation—to be seen—six years earlier, when he'd climbed the water tower in Morgantown one night to spray paint his and Shawna's names, had scaled that skinny, creaking ladder after she, during one of their arguments, accused him of possessing not one romantic bone in his body, of lacking all spontaneity, of defining love the way he defined probabilities. He would, he decided, show her. Breathlessly, he committed his minor vandalism, legs unsteady, his hands shaking. In his haste, in his constant looking down and shivering through his vertigo and hearing police sirens and bullhorns and footsteps on the ladder (none of which came, the night silent and breezy), he'd inadvertently misspelled his own name: WEMER LOVES SHAWNA. He hadn't noticed until the next day, at the same time she did, when he'd driven her out to see it.

She'd smiled, breathed a little laugh through her nose. "It's sweet, though, honey. It really is." They sat on the warm hood of his car looking up. Weimer cursed a second time at his mistake, retracing his steps, trying to think how he could have missed a letter.

"It's scary up there," he told her. "You don't realize how high it is."

She cupped his cheek and let her eyes move over his face. They'd been married for four years, had lived through the death of her mother and two early miscarriages. How could he fault her for wanting a little buoyant romance to balance out all that dark and heavy-laden love?

She'd worn her hair shoulder length, then, and had to keep

tucking it behind her ears. "You see the irony here, though, don't you?" she said.

"I commit the big act and screw it up, right? Next time I break the law, I'll get every detail perfect, okay?" He picked at the dried paint on the backs of his knuckles.

She closed her eyes, briefly. "*Next* time, leave out the 'M' or the 'R.' " She shook her head. "Don't you *see*? You just illustrated what I've been saying for four years. 'I' is missing. You." She tapped his chest. "*I*. See?"

Weimer looked back up at the fuzzy black letters, high above the town.

Shawna reached up, rubbed his cheek with her thumb. "Just how you are, right? I mean, tell anyone we know that 'I' is missing from your declarations of love, and all they'll question is your grammar."

Then, like all things, that day passed and faded. Things seemed fine. Six years went by, filtered through the familiar. Shawna began making the ceramic serving platters and place settings in bulk, production work, racks and racks of them in her basement studio, and selling them steadily. (He asked her once why she'd quit making the sunflower fish sculptures she'd made in grad school; she only shrugged and said that the place settings were what sold.) And they had their baby now, a girl seven months old, little and pink and mewling, who Shawna kept between them in bed at night so that his sleep was mostly a vague awareness of not rolling over. The baby ("She has a *name*," Shawna had said, just before he'd left for Utah) had been mostly Shawna's enterprise, another project she'd taken on and sometimes invited him to look at. Things had evened out at work and he taught his intro physics and calculus classes from yellowing notes, happy that he didn't teach current events, that the basic facts of calc and physics never changed. And then one day he had a conversation with a young woman about a mutual student. She had dark, wet eyes, that small gap in her teeth, and she asked him if he wanted to go get a beer. He hesitated only half a second before saying okay.

Now, in the wan and chilly desert, Weimer wondered at the smallness of moments, how the fuckups can turn on so insignificant a thing, ushered in by a pair of syllables thoughtlessly uttered, or by an "I" missing from a water tank. Weimer shook the rattle can and sprayed a big Day-Glo **OK**, the word that had brought him so much trouble, on the left rear fender, then X'd it out. He sprayed that missing **I** right in the middle of the trunk. A little life revision, by proxy.

They finished the Impala in swoops and whirls of orange and green, spraying over the rust holes and dents, the paint staining their fingertips. Still, Lisk would not say what plans he had for the car, only that the new day would inform. As his final act of mystery for the night, Lisk pulled from the trunk a broom, a roll of duct tape, and a cinder block, setting these on the dusty front seat. A TV magician, readying some elaborate stage illusion.

Inside, their house was done mostly in books and Wal-Mart furniture—pressboard shelves, beanbag chairs, a couch covered with a bedspread. Weimer was touched by how ragtag and undergrad it looked, how impermanent. But Lisk and Maysoon had more permanence than any couple he knew. He watched them now, sitting in a room that lacked a TV, lacked a coffee table, lacked a pile of magazines featuring cake recipes and diet plans. Maysoon knelt behind Lisk and carefully combed out his thin rope of hair, her small, hard muscles moving as she brushed and rebraided. They had been together close to twelve years, had moved at least half a dozen times to increasingly remote areas of the country, cut off from the restaurants and malls and grocery stores that in Weimer's mind anchored a regular life. They were like the Japanese high-rises he taught his sophomores about, built to twist and flex so as to withstand earthquakes. Maybe that was it. His own existence—his and Shawna's—had been too rigid, and thus prone to early destruction.

At 4:00 A.M. things grew quiet, and after drunkenly calculating the three-hour time difference, Weimer decided to call Shawna, knowing he would catch her just up, bathrobe belted tightly around her waist, sitting at the kitchen stool reading the paper and drinking tea.

"So you run away and get drunk with the Mormons," she said, after answering on the third ring. As it turned out she'd still been asleep, after a bad night with the baby.

"Lisk isn't Mormon," he said, and right away it was going badly. Then again, what did he expect? He watched Lisk and Maysoon in the next room, asleep on the couch under a blanket.

"Right. An anarchist among the latter-day saints. I forgot."

They both fell quiet. Her words skimmed close to old jokes between them about Lisk, whom they'd both known since grad school, only there was no joking in her voice now.

"So what are you doing?" he said, realizing how anemic this sounded. *How's it going? What's up?* "I mean, how are you getting along?"

"I nurse Annie and torch stoneware, same as always." He could almost hear her shrug. "You aren't the only one who gets bored with the view, you know. Difference is, I don't try to improve the landscape by digging it up and planting land mines."

"Shawna, I'm sorry."

She sighed. "Yeah, you mentioned that before you took off."

"You *wanted* me to take off. That's why I left."

He voice rose sharply. "I never told you to *leave,* to run *away* from us."

He hesitated, feeling stupid, exposed. "You never said not to."

"Ah, *God,*" she said and gave a short laugh. "That's a big damn list, Andrew, of the things I never said *not* to do." In their long history she called him "Andrew" only when she felt particularly angry or particularly affectionate. Now he tried to hear pieces of both, as if the edges of her love and her anger could follow opposite orbits and eventually overlap. The night he climbed the tower ladder—rust biting the palms of his hands, spasms in his legs—a stiff breeze had swayed the tower in slow arcs, a walking giant shouldering him, and he'd stood on the grated catwalk, hanging onto the rail, looking out over the matrix of light that netted the city. Earlier that afternoon, he'd shown his summer school class a PBS documentary. *The Unifying Theory of Everything,* about the efforts of Hawking and Kaku and the others to mate relativity and quantum theory. A failed effort thus far, like the medievalist physicians mating rabbits and badgers. Sitting in the darkened classroom with his half-sleeping students, he understood that he had only a little better grasp on this material than they did, that he was just another drudge watching television, that he hadn't kept up, had sacrificed his knowledge and research at the altar of steadfastness.

But as he stood there on that water tower, he remembered this much: Research was intuition, an outcome could be felt before it could be demonstrated. He'd spread his arms wide above the city and felt his own everything beneath him, a lifetime of outcomes. Shawna and their four-year marriage; his job at Bishop McGuiness; the polite distancing of in-laws and parents; his ten-year-old Honda Accord; a rented apartment near the college; the bathroom mirror that showed him a fledgling bald spot; the quiet sadness that followed the two miscarriages, when he'd held her for hours, her chin tucked into his collarbone as she cried into the cup formed by his neck and shoulder. The losses had pulled a hole in the center of their lives, a dark sloping tube that funneled them into each other, until time had spread wide the tapered edges and pushed them back into the flatness of daily life. He'd leaned on the rail, looking down upon the whole of his life, devoid of mystery, unified by little more than his own existence. He wanted to love it, tried to. But Lisk was right, he *had* opted for triviality, traded his talent for an unadorned life, for a unifying theory of nothing. Then he'd spray painted his mustered-up romance for that life, leaving himself out of it.

He sighed into the phone. "What do you want from me, Shawna?" he asked.

"I want you to tell me why men go to all the trouble to construct decent lives for themselves, then do everything they can to dismantle them."

"I wouldn't say every man does that."

"You're right. It's not really a law, more a probability. Does that help you understand?"

"Shawna . . ."

"Come home, Andy," she said. "We're all stretched out over eight states. Just, please . . . come home."

"But . . . what are we doing? I mean, come home and *what?*"

"Park the car. Lock the door. Kiss your daughter."

"Kiss my wife?"

"No—"

A ripple of panic gripped his stomach. "You see? So what's the point?"

"The *point* is that you have work to do. Heavy lifting of everything you undid." The baby began crying in the background. "You know what? Your whole problem since the start is that you think you can be in this marriage, but not *really* in it. Like love is this toy train you get to wind up once in a while and send around the track. It gives you a laugh, it—"

"Shawna . . ."

"Shut *up*." He'd never heard her so angry. That was how his brain, his good, dependable brain, formed the words: *I've never heard her so angry.* That was the best it could do, a cliché in the face of his life unraveling. When he left she'd been sad and quiet, and now his absence had given her sadness room to grow, to bulk up into anger.

"You are going to learn." She hesitated, breathed. "I don't care if I have to make you write it five hundred times, our marriage is not a goddamn toy train. I want you to *hear* me."

"I do. I hear you."

She was quiet a few long seconds. The baby made gurgling sounds, Shawna holding her now. "You know what it is, Andy?" she said, calmer now. "It's a *real* train. It's a Mack truck. And if you don't know what I mean by that, or *can't* know, we're done." She wasn't even crying. There was no dampness or mush to her words, only that quiet snap, a lightly balled fist. He told himself he deserved no less.

Those Imagined Lives

. . .

After the phone call he spent three hours sitting up in a chair, dozing. At one point he woke up and walked out onto the deck, surprised at the chill in the air, and bent to look through the eyepiece of Maysoon's Dob. He saw only the blackness of empty space (he liked to impress this on his students, that three quarters of the universe was a vacuum, made of nothing), until he pivoted the telescope on its base and the gibbous moon filled his vision, so bright and sudden that he took a step back. The clarity of its pocked landscape, its craters and oceans of dust, moved him so, he had to look away and draw a breath. Somehow it made him sad, in a way the phone call hadn't. If he'd been a poet or even a gifted enough physicist, he might have fashioned the metaphor: himself . . . the moon, a satellite to his own place of origin, cold and distant and dead, but always, always falling toward home. Did that work? He imagined Shawna's reaction to the idea, to his romanticizing his own detachment, making a big, sad moon of his remoteness. Sometimes when they made love, Shawna would grab his hair in both hands and pull his face down to hers, eyes to eyes, forcing his gaze down on her. Here is where metaphor fell apart, he thought, as he sat on the couch and wrapped himself in the blanket. The moon's distant gaze never failed, and if you pulled it down, it would kill us all.

Lisk woke him with coffee and a shove. Weimer had fallen asleep on the deck, and his clothes were full of dew, like sequins, his head not as bad as he'd feared it would be. Maysoon stood puffy-eyed in the kitchen, making pecan pancakes, singing to herself. As they ate, Weimer could tell that Lisk was hyped up. He kept downing coffee, darting his eyes as he chewed, rubbing his hands on his camo pants, talking too much about nothing.

"The big boy gets wired, doesn't he?" Maysoon said, smiling.

"Come *on*," Lisk said. "It gets too late in the day and we'll have to worry about those fuckers out racing their cars."

"Who?" Weimer said. "Where?"

"On the salt flats. Lawyers with their Volvos, playing race car." He poked at the orange juice carton with his fork. "Let's get moving."

Lisk stacked the dishes in the sink while Maysoon pulled a gun case from under the couch. Inside was the old prototype of the machine gun Lisk had sold to the Saudis, along with a nickel-plated shotgun and several handguns, large caliber from what Weimer knew. These they carried out and set in the backseat of Lisk's other car, an old Ford Bronco he'd had forever, which at some point he'd made into a convertible by cutting off the top with a chainsaw. They checked fluids on the Bronco and the Impala.

"So we're going hunting?" Weimer said. "That's your surprise? You disappoint me, Lisk." In grad school once or twice Lisk had dragged him into the woods to shoot at turkeys, and Weimer had never liked it. Too cold, too early in the morning, too wet and messy.

"Yeah, you tell me an hour from now if you're disappointed or not."

Weimer nodded. "Speaking of disappointment . . ." he said, and proceeded to tell Lisk about his drunken phone call with Shawna.

They walked over to the Impala. Lisk dug the block, tape, and broom from the front seat. "Hate to tell you, but our little Shawna is right on, daddy," he said. "It just ain't love unless it takes up *residence*. You know?"

"I guess I don't know. I guess that's my problem."

"That's the *why* of our baby, man. You should know this by now, too. Refocusing, okay? You think a long, hard while about crib death, and see if that don't put a fine point on your familial love."

Weimer watched as Lisk levered the broom through the steering wheel and wedged it against the windshield, handle sticking out the window. He strapped everything in place with duct tape—the broom, the window, the steering wheel.

"Duct tape is our most constant friend," Lisk said.

"You mind telling me what the hell you're doing? What are we hunting out here anyway? Scorpions? Snakes?"

"Impalas," Lisk said. "We're hunting Chevrolets today, bro."

"*What*—" As he watched Lisk prop the cinder block against the gas pedal of the car, he understood. The Impala pointed straight out into the salt flats, miles of which lay behind the house like baked snow, like the landscape of a distant planet. Before Weimer could say another word, Lisk leaned in and started the car, the engine rumbling the ground beneath them, then stepped back. He reached quickly through the window again and punched the shifter into drive. The car shot away from them, fishtailed, veered off a little to the left before rocketing out into all that flat and white. The engine wound to a high whine, a burning blue haze left behind, stinging his nostrils.

"You have completely lost your mind," Weimer said, his voice unsteady, hangover finally finding him.

In response, Lisk pulled the pistol from his belt, took slow aim, and fired, shattering the car's back windshield. "It's wounded," he said. "All we have to do is track it and kill it." He unwrapped a piece of gum and stuck it in his mouth.

Weimer followed Lisk to the Bronco, and they took off after it, Maysoon sitting on the back porch reading the paper. She gave them a distracted wave. By now the Impala was only a faint, Day-Glo smudge against the expanse of white, like a balloon disappearing into the sky. They roared off after it, Lisk grinding through gears, pushing the Bronco up to eighty-five. Weimer started to tremble, his stomach churning. The wind and sand tore at their faces, the engine a loud hum, Weimer squinting, hands gripping the rattling doorframe. Lisk reached across the backseat and handed Weimer the nickel-plated shotgun.

"You've used one before," he shouted, leaning toward Weimer, his words blunted by the wind. "Hard to miss." He gave Weimer a thumbs-up and smiled, his lips caked and dry. They were gaining on the Impala, which raced on blindly, two plumes of white trailing it. Weimer could think only of all the highways he'd crossed driving up, all those families in vans, of the lawyers in Volvos Lisk had mentioned, of some lone house, like Lisk's own, stuck out here on the rim of nothing.

"Go ahead and fire it once, get used to it," Lisk said, leaning toward him. When Weimer hesitated, Lisk used his free hand to hoist the gun to Weimer's shoulder. "Go on. Fire the damn thing. Mazel tov."

Weimer sighted down the shining barrel, but what was the point of aiming? He was only firing into the emptiness, shooting at nothing. He pumped, pulled the trigger, and watched the salt explode in a long white feather as his shoulder throbbed with recoil. Lisk whooped and slapped his knee, fired the pistol twice into the air. They rode without speaking as Weimer tried to calculate just how far they'd gone.

"Hey, listen," Lisk shouted, lifting his voice over the wind. "This whole Shawna thing, you need to *listen* to her." He spoke as if they were sitting around the table on the deck drinking beer. "It's like your *job*, man—"

"Don't start," Weimer said. "'Macrocosm, triviality.' You made your point fifteen years ago." He spat the salty grit from his tongue.

"You want the truth, bro?" He leaned down farther, out of the wind. "You didn't opt for triviality, you opted for smallness."

This was the second critique of his personality in less than six hours, and Weimer felt impatient with it. "Same thing," he shouted.

"Yeah, like 'Spain' and 'nipple' are the same thing." Lisk shook his head. "Hold the wheel." He let go of the steering wheel, and Weimer had no choice but to grab it. Lisk leaned up over the windshield and fired three rounds at the Impala. He sat down heavily, stomped the gas pedal. "Shit, we aren't even close."

But they were closer. Weimer could just make out his own swirly paint lines down the side of the car, the **OK** he'd crossed out on the rear fender. The blazing orange and green of the car, the yellow-white streaks of sun flashing off the windows, all of it looked lunatic out there in the white flats. A mirage, some tight-wound dream.

"Listen, Andy," Lisk said, slowing to make himself heard. "You were afraid of the big job—competition, keeping up—so you took the small job. Same deal, you're afraid of the big family dotted line where you sign it all away in piss and blood and money, so what? You go find yourself a little piece on the side."

A *piece on the side,* Weimer thought, remembering his earlier efforts to name his transgression. He shook his head, eyes full of grit. "And that was careful and safe?" His eyes burned.

"Hell, yes." Lisk turned the wheel hard to come up on the Impala at an angle. "You'd have a little fun, Shawna would get a little mad, then you'd say a little apology."

Weimer winced at the near truth of this. What he'd *really* thought was that over time—before Christmas, he'd imagined— the whole thing would evaporate, and Shawna would never know.

"Am I right?" Lisk said.

He nodded. "Something like that."

"But it goes the other way, and our little Shawna pulls a Godzilla on you, right? Or was it a Harpo Marx? It's always one or the other."

He didn't answer but sat thinking, absently fingering the gun barrel and rubbing his eyes. Lisk whipped hard right, downshifted, and punched the gas, leaning forward in his seat. When Weimer looked up, they were next to the Impala, right alongside it at ninety miles per hour. The air was burned oil, heat off a griddle. Lisk let out a whoop and edged closer, the Impala an orange-and-green vibration. Weimer put his hand out to catch the powder spewing up. The big **I** he'd painted on the trunk shone garishly in the sun. Lisk swerved closer still, so that Weimer could have reached out his shaking fingers and run them along the dried drips of paint. His breathing came quick in the shallow of his lungs. They would crash, twist end over end with the Impala, and no one would find them out here, ever. Then Lisk backed off far enough to raise his pistol, hold it out across

Weimer, and shatter the side window. Bits of glass rattled inside
the car, and Lisk fired again, putting a gaping hole through the
door. Weimer thought about dying out in the desert, dying so
stupidly, trying to hunt a car.

And he thought about going home. About what Shawna had
said: Park the car, lock the door, kiss Annie. And then—what?
The years ahead loomed as blank white and featureless as the
desert salt around him. He thought of that night on the water
tower, the whole frail world, for once, under him, within his view,
his legs and hands shaking as he took it all in, the stars and clouds,
the grid of light, Shawna down there somewhere, that dark
tube of their grief still closed all around them. . . . He shut his
eyes, felt the spray can in his hand, the sway of the tower, the
wind pushing a part into his hair . . . felt something else he
could almost see, that was almost in his vision.

Then Lisk downshifted, pressed the gas, and slipped in front
of the Impala. If they stopped suddenly—a blowout, a dead
engine—the other car would push right over them, plow them
into the salt. Lisk looked backward through the open top of the
Bronco, raised his pistol, and took out the windshield, shattering it.

"Here I'm hogging the fun," Lisk shouted. "You, bro. Gas
tank or radiator, your choice. Either one will bring her down."

Weimer shook his head. "If I shoot the gas tank," he shouted,
"the whole thing will explode and us with it."

Lisk laughed. "Man, too many fucking movies. Take out the
tank, the car *stops*. No fuel, dude. So what'll it be?"

Weimer just wanted this over with. "The tank, I guess," he
said. He pumped the shotgun. Lisk slowed, swerved, and came
up behind the Impala again. Weimer leaned out into the wind

and raised the gun to his shoulder, aiming this time, sighting straight down to where the license plate should have been.

"Go on, man, take her out," Lisk said.

Weimer held as steady as he could in the shaking truck and let his finger brush the trigger, but did not fire. He tried for a moment to imagine what the life of the Impala had been, how it was once a real car with a real family riding in its seats, carrying some man off to work in the morning, his briefcase on the floor-board beside him, or some woman to pick up her children after band practice, way back in 1973 when the car, those imagined lives, were still shiny and new. He could see them piled in together, kids spotting out-of-state license plates or arguing over the radio dial, the mother handing around peanut butter sandwiches, the father stopping at toll booths, and he felt a momentary shame at what they'd made the car into, a garish, graffitied, hunted wreck, broken under the hot gape of the desert sun. But, at the same time, the car looked so random and colorful, so determined as it raced toward nothing but its own end, that it seemed to him then a beautiful thing—so stark and sad and absolute in its demise that while Lisk whooped and hollered beside him and the sun and a million planets shone down on him, when Weimer finally did pull the trigger, the only thing he could feel was a small and insignificant grief.

St. Jimmy

Saint Jimmy tell me they name the river for him, tell me he own the river, tell me he let everybody travel his water. Shopping cart squeak when my thumbs touch it, one wheel bad. Cart full up of rust and fish scales. Saint Jimmy lean way out to breathe blue smoke, boats stirring his river. Saint Jimmy say, Breathe that good air. Water mend itself when they pass. Electric cables move in the wind, throw off sparks everywhere. Big iron building cough up more boats, bridge split to let them go. Croakers haul up on the wire and I throw them in the cart, flapping blood. A hundred suns burn gray and yellow from a glass wall, tall building color of bad pennies and shrimp. People there wearing Easter clothes, swimming river smells. Night wind like bobcats, cables snap blue and green around the sky, drop fire in the river, drop fire off our pier. Fire everywhere. Saint Jimmy wear

his hat the way God want him to, cough and the cable fire running through him hard, lead his breathing to ruin. River turns
black ribbon leaking moon, making up cold, moaning and
groaning. Saint Jimmy say, There ain't no fire, that's in your
head. He say, Be quiet and lay down and go to sleep.

Oil smell fill up our mouth. Saint Jimmy say he big hungry, he
gas-tank hungry, throwing K-1 on the Sterno cans, hauling up
croakers on the wire. Cut them up on my knife, let them die in
the fire. Save the insides, always save the insides. Sheet boats
dance around pretty and sleepy. Lean out to grab one and Saint
Jimmy say, Fool, say, Sit down here and eat. Saint Jimmy stuff
news in my sleeves, say, You smell worse than this fish. Big
bridge split open and stop all the trucks. Saint Jimmy say, That's
everything like a woman. Bridge make a noise and let the trucks
go through. Saint Jimmy say, She all done now, she don't wait
for me. He laugh and show his teeth. He say, Don't you got no
sense a humor? Flannel men carry out poles, pull fish out of
Saint Jimmy's river. He say he let them, say, Don't you get no
ideas, you leave them folks alone. Saint Jimmy cough out cable
fire, it hurting him bad. Wind take cold from the river and give
it to us, make the electric cables slap on their crosses. Crosses
up to the sky everywhere. Fire. Hum grow like a weed. Men
hand us a dollar and smokes. All clean faces. Saint Jimmy say, I
give you a dollar for more smokes. They laugh with all their
teeth. Saint Jimmy say, Don't mind him, say, He schizo, say, He
ain't got no sense a humor, either. Say, If I had another dollar I
might buy him one. I tell them this Saint Jimmy's river, they say,
That's right, friend. Saint Jimmy give me his bad eye, say, Don't

think what you thinking, say, They might put you back where you come from. Cables hit like fish, the sun eat up their fire. Saint Jimmy got his breathing led to ruin. Make me want to cry.

When the men leave the sun move around. Water settle out smooth and change color, no sheet boats, no dancing. Blue smoke boats run home unzipping the river. Saint Jimmy lean out to breathe, say, Put a fire on. Sun break up like oil, settle on the bad penny building. Saint Jimmy wave up at the lights, at shadow people, say, Don't stand there like a statue. Say, Me and you hook baiters and masturbators. Say, When you ever going to laugh? Fire going, haul up croakers on a wire. Saint Jimmy raise a bottle in a net, say, You stop that noise. Swallow bones and fish. Bad penny building eat up a hundred suns for dinner, wind move the cables on their crosses, drop fire off our pier. Saint Jimmy say, They use too much steel, everything a waste. Bridge quiet and black, river leaking sky. Saint Jimmy say, Go to sleep, then a man walk out, dressed in the river. He kick Saint Jimmy, touching him hard all over. Saint Jimmy buried in his arms, say, Don't have nothing. River water whisper my ear. Man put his foot in Saint Jimmy's neck. Knife find my hand, slice croakers in the fire. Saint Jimmy's teeth scrape cement, mouth all in blood. Oil blood. Man bend down, say, Tempt me, say, Nobody in this world miss you. Saint Jimmy's eyes burning, lungs breathing out cable fire. Wind go hide, crosses bless the river. Saint Jimmy say, Yessir, you right on everything. Knife own my arm and haul me up, shad gone steel and swimming. Man say, Who's your dummy friend? Saint Jimmy swivel his bad eye at me, say, Don't do nothing but sit back down. Knife on my leg, man's breath in clouds. Could slice him up in the fire. Clouds put a sweat on me. Saint Jimmy say, Not what you thinking. Man grab the bottle and move his foot, Saint Jimmy fill up, teeth dripping. Man walk away where he came. Wind done hiding, push blue fire off the cables. Knife made of sugar now. Wire cart full of cold, rust dropping, bad wheel. Saint Jimmy say, Where you going, sit your ass down. Say, That man like a little fly, land on shit once, then gone. I tell I had him good. Saint Jimmy say, Throw that meanness in the river, say, They put you back where you come from. I tell that man just like a blind-eye fish, we should throw back to the river. Saint Jimmy laugh blood, say, I get to keep my dollar.

Wake up in black sky, fire licking in tongues. Cables snap, river water moaning. Fire throw out around the bridge, knit up the sky, make a hum. Saint Jimmy say, You quit that now and be quiet, say, We never should a lost that bottle. He put his hands on me, fire sucked up like a straw. Everything steel but his hands. Cables hit and make sparks that fall to river cold. Saint Jimmy say, Smell that, say, That put a cough in me sure as I'm living. He shake and rub his teeth. Bridge flash red, make us red. Saint Jimmy say, Look that old bitch winking at us, won't open her legs. Cough rip him, pull him down like it got its foot in his neck. He sit up, rub dark oil in his hands, say, We need a bottle. Iron boat sit, a hole in the black. Wind shoot from the hole and find us. Saint Jimmy say, Jesus we'll die, chatter broken teeth. Cables push a fire that hitch the wind right through. Saint Jimmy glow like coals, cough scars inside. His middle all burning him out. He say, If we had a woman.

St. Jimmy

. . .

Saint Jimmy got his arms in the sun, stand on the rail. He breathe blue. He drink and throw me a half-gone bottle. Go in me cool fire, paper in my clothes make me big. Saint Jimmy dance the rail, wind grab his pants. Cough bend him and he drink and move. Saint Jimmy say, No hands, say, This rail don't own me. Say, What I need's a new suit. Sheet boat tip over, water shake around, rail bend with his shoes. Saint Jimmy cough and the bottle come out red. He say, Get the wire in the water. Steel wire haul up empty. Saint Jimmy say, Give them a stomach, they eat their own kind. Fish all gone, cart empty. Saint Jimmy say, Croakers is like money, got to have it to get it. Rail make a sound and Saint Jimmy on the cement, say, I know all about falling. Drink and cough. Drink. Wind falling asleep and the cables make a song, whisper. Saint Jimmy say, We got to eat or the cold eat us. Pull through the cart, plastic and paper, throw-away razors and tin. Legs go to sleep without him. Saint Jimmy say, Where's that knife? Pull it from me and my hand get cold. Saint Jimmy peel off his skin, dripping red. Bottle red. Say, Look like a worm, don't it, say, Don't lose that, I got to eat that. Haul up croaker on a wire. Throw K-1 on the Sterno and cut it up. Wrap his hand in a paper. Saint Jimmy smile broken teeth, say, Hush up that noise, it'll grow back. Saint Jimmy say, What you do without me?

Night getting fast. Bridge wink and split her legs. Bad penny building eat its suns. Nobody live there. River a long black hole, grow iron buildings and bury up the moon. Trucks on the bridge throw yellow and green. Saint Jimmy lower the bottle in a net, say, Don't get thirsty yet. Hone the knife on my shoe. Throw out a stomach, haul up croaker on a wire. Saint Jimmy say, Put it in the bank. Throw in the cart flapping blood. Bridge groan its last closing. Wind come up big, pull water off the river and hit us, raining backward. Saint Jimmy wrap me in plastic from the cart, say, We got to keep you fresh, case you die. Say, Damn, I done spent that dollar. Saint Jimmy wrap himself in plastic, throw paper on the Sterno. Say, Go to sleep. My eyes won't listen.

River, bridge, building, pier. Me. Saint Jimmy. Night, night, everything a quilt on tar, bubbling up. Tar drip down black. Hot put a boil in the river, black noise. Pull up on the cart, hot melt my hands to it. Drunk wind falling down everywhere and moaning. Lay down with it in plastic, still moaning. Saint Jimmy in plastic, oil leak out of him. Fire show his bones right through. Bridge make us red, trucks draw a line yellow and green. Crosses taller than everything, a thousand feet high and signs warning away. Electrified and humming. Cables twist like eels. River moaning and wind moaning afraid. Saint Jimmy in plastic and the cough right through him. Say his name. Touch Saint Jimmy and I hear him break, fire put out and liquid smoke. Skin gone hard and the moaning won't quit. Moaning. Wind peel blue fire off the cables, yellow sparks like sunflowers. Fire seeds carry. Blue lightning off the crosses arc the sky, hit the bridge a wet burning and drip off in the river. Black water full of sparks. Moaning. Glow the water, lights in a fog. Sky melt in smoke and rain, bounce fire off our pier. Pop and make a smell. Fire in Saint

St. Jimmy

Jimmy run through him to dark. Everything broken and I tell I need him back. River die and a million pink fish float up. Bridge go limp and trucks tumble in, make a ripple on the dead water. Waves on oil. Hold Saint Jimmy and the hard wind catch my plastic. Plastic float up away from me like ash.

Beneath the Deep, Slow Motion

Early morning, and Clarendon starts like a wind-up toy—cotton and rice farmers machining the Delta soil, jackhammers breaking the streets downtown. Bosco is talking, too much and too loud, finding no difference between nighttime talk and daytime, between drunk and sober. Along the shore, the streetlights blink out all at once. For the second time that morning, Bosco talks about killing Leo Myer.

"We could, Ray," he says, sober a moment. "You know we could."

Ray feels something shift when the words are said, feels that slow, familiar movement toward trouble.

"Always running off at the goddamn mouth, Bosco," Ray says, laughs it off. "Ought to wrap it with duct tape instead of this."

Ray waves his twelve gauge, its stock covered in greasy tape, then shoves the barrel under the river's surface and pulls the trigger. The muffled *whomp* boils downward, jarring his bones, the water exploding upward in a rain of mud and algae. Bubbles rise with the blood and mangled remains of a carp. Ray nets it from the water, tosses it in the cooler. Later, he will grill it over hardware cloth with potatoes wrapped in tinfoil, and they will pick out like bones from the flesh the tiny lead pellets, spitting them into the currents.

"You say that 'cause you know I'm right," Bosco says, his smile cutting thin, framed by the mustache that edges his mouth. They have been up all night, drinking beer and shooting carp. Ray switches off the lamps that float in the shallows. The carp move in shadows across the pebbly bottom. Bosco finishes his chocolate milk, drops the carton and stomps it, making Ray jump.

"About all I know is you're a kid, Bosco," Ray says. "A thirty-five-year-old goddamn kid." Bosco shrugs and drinks, his shirtless chest bony and sunken.

They stand on the deck of Bosco's houseboat, which once served as a repair barge and welding deck for BG Ironworks until it ran on a shoal in the middle of the White River, fifty yards downstream of the railroad trestle outside Clarendon. Permanent as an island now, the boat holds as the river washes around it. Red-winged blackbirds balance on the rope that connects the barge to shore, the same rope that Ray and Bosco shinny across for groceries, liquor, and generator fuel. When Bosco finds women from town they shinny across with him, legs scissoring, skirts gaping, Ray shining his flashlight on the whites of their thighs. The women squeal and curse Bosco for where he lives, curse the light and the oily rope, drunk and laughing while Ray holds his breath, waiting for them to slip and disappear forever beneath the deep, slow motion of the river.

Bosco lifts another beer from the plastic bag hanging in the current. The white scar from his surgery looks fresh still, lines stitched across his shoulder where the Jonesboro doctors removed the cancer. The indentations there form notches in the line of his shoulder, the flesh gouged and ridged. Ray looks at it, winces. After the surgery was when he began to spend all his time on the barge—not just Saturday nights—helping Bosco tie his shoes, cook his food, and, for a time, button his pants.

Bosco takes the gun, his mouth hanging open as he scans the water. They will shoot until the sheriff's deputy drives down to the riverbank and hollers for them to call it a day.

"We better quit soon," Ray says.

"How much you think them diamonds are worth?" Bosco asks. "How easy would it be to walk in there, off the sonofabitch, and get out?" He drinks his beer and elbows Ray, starts humming the *Jeopardy* theme. Riffing off game shows is a stage in Bosco's drunkenness, lodged somewhere between vomiting and blacking out. After they have caught a day's haul of oysters, he will watch the shows on his little five-inch black-and-white, the cord for the TV running off the generator inside the cramped cabin of the barge, where he keeps his mattress, refrigerator, and the old issues of *National Geographic* he finds on the library free table and uses for kindling. Nights they sit at the edge of the barge, occupying an old couch Bosco found on the roadside and floated across, left in the sun to dry. Bosco watches game shows and comedies, shouts at the screen, while Ray watches the river and thinks about the water flowing past them, all the bits of sediment carried to the ocean. They sit until the generator runs out of gas, then fire up lamps to shoot carp in the shallows, run trotlines for catfish.

"Just let the idea go, Bosco," Ray tells him.

"You don't think I'd do it?"

"Well, let's see. Last month, panning for gold was gonna make us rich and before that crystal meth and before that parting out cars. Now it's hauling oysters that's not making us dime one, so you're going to kill Leo Myer and take a bunch of diamonds that might or might not even be there. Bullshit, Bosco."

Bosco takes back the gun, racks it, and fires beneath the water. Bits of gravel clink against the side of the rusted water heater that floats beside them, chained to the barge.

"One big difference this time, Ray," Bosco says. "I *need* the goddamn money." He blinks and looks away, tips up his beer can to hide his eyes.

The first time the doctor found the cancer in Bosco's shoulder was an accident, an X-ray done after some bar-fight soreness wouldn't work itself out. With no money or insurance, Bosco had worked out a payment plan that would see him through to old age, and if he skipped even one payment, Ray knew, the collection agency would be along to take his barge, his beaten-down truck, his little TV, his refrigerator, and his last pair of socks. Now he complains of new soreness in his shoulder, tiredness in his days, but his joke is that he can't buy any more sickness until the last one is paid for. He has stopped smiling when he says it.

Bosco tosses his beer can into the river and fires at it. He racks and fires again, at the willow tree that tethers the shinny rope. Ray grabs the gun by the barrel and twists it from Bosco's fingers. He spits into the water and watches it float away, then ejects the empty shell.

"We won't ever be rich, Bosco, not in this life."

They cook and eat carp into the afternoon, putting off that day's haul of oysters, work which renders their only cash until the end of the month when Ray collects for his weekend motor route. He drives the same camper truck he sleeps in when he's not on the barge, muscling it down bumpy washouts in the dead of night, listening to radio baseball and talk shows, shoving the *Clarendon Gazette* into the green plastic tubes mounted at the side of the road. All day, while they eat and drink, while the river washes around them, Bosco talks of Leo's diamonds, how they are there for the taking, how that woman he met at the bar has seen them herself. He talks nonstop, nodding and jabbering, rubbing his ruined shoulder.

By early evening Ray lets himself be talked into a visit to Leo's place. Bosco says he wants to case it out, words he's lifted from some TV show. Ray agrees, wanting Bosco to stand there in Leo's apartment, work it through his brain, see the impossibility of it. They drive out County Road 10 toward Berryville, drinking beer, swatting mosquitoes. They come to the brick building that once held Sunshine Dairy, where Leo runs his business from a single room on the second floor. Out beside the road is Leo's handpainted sign advertising palm reading, tarot cards, and shiatsu massages, ten dollars each. The front windows are webbed by strips of masking tape and yellowed, curling posters for the Shriner's Bar-B-Q and the Marv-L Circus. Inside, the old cream separators and capping machines sit rusting, covered in dust.

"So if Leo's rich, how come he lives in this hole?" Ray asks.

"You've heard the story," Bosco says.

"Yeah, I've heard it," Ray says. "That one and about a thousand others."

"Well, I guess we'll see, then, won't we?"

The story seeps into the bars in the way of all rumor, through spilled beer and bullshit and games of eight ball and last call, places where Bosco has picked up the story and made it his own. The word is that Leo Myer once worked as a diamond wholesaler in Atlanta, that one afternoon he pocketed five pounds of rough stones off the plane from Barrons, that he picked Clarendon, Arkansas, off a road atlas and settled in to hide himself. Leo speaks with a New York accent, wears flowing caftans to the IGA in town, silver rings and ear hoops, tiny braids woven in his longish hair.

"That's right, Bosco," Ray says. "We'll see, and then you can drop this shit."

"Just keep his ass busy," Bosco says.

After a steep climb to the second floor, they ring the buzzer. The door opens with a tinkling of chimes and Leo yawns at them from behind his graying beard. Behind him, the TV plays a commercial for dog food.

"Visitors," he says. The room is thick with incense and yellow light, the walls pale green, hung with feathers and beads. "What can I do for you boys?" He is without his caftan and earrings, and wears instead sweatpants and a gray T-shirt.

"My buddy here would like his palm read," Bosco says.

"Is that a fact? Just what problem are you working through?"

Ray shrugs. "Whatever."

Leo smiles at them. "Why don't you fellows save your money. Go buy a few rounds at the Barbary Coast."

"No, we really want to know the future," Bosco says. "We can pay." He cuts his eyes at Ray as he unfolds a crumpled ten from his jeans and hands it to Leo.

Leo shrugs, opens the door to let them in. They sit down at a pocked wooden table in the kitchen while Bosco heads toward the sink.

"Mind if I get some water?" Bosco asks. Leo waves the back of his hand and slips on a pair of dime store reading glasses. He uses the remote control to click off the TV.

"Why don't you tell me what you're thinking," Leo says to Ray. "That's our usual start."

"I was thinking how much this dump looks like a whore-house," Ray says. He watches Bosco drink from a jelly jar.

"This anger toward me interests me," Leo says. He looks up, smiles, touches his beard. "Is that what you paid for? To come here and vent?"

"Ray's just nervous," Bosco says from behind Leo. "His first time."

Leo holds out his fingertips as if he's asking Ray for a dance. Bosco nods, and Ray offers his hand. Leo's fingers are warm and damp. He bends Ray's hand toward the light, caressing the palm. Bosco walks slowly around the room touching the strings of colored beads, the macramé wall decorations, the feathers hung from threads. Ray doesn't like a man touching him. He drinks with his left hand, downing his beer.

"Anger is bad for your heart, as bad as cigarettes," Leo says. "The Chinese call anger a weary bird with no place to roost."

Bosco slips to the back of the room and eases open a drawer on a rolltop desk. Ray imagines he hears it squeak. He watches Bosco riffle through papers with his thumb, then pull a wooden cigar box from the back of the drawer. Leo moves as if to look over his shoulder.

"That's me exactly," Ray says quickly. "All pissed off and no place to go."

"I see that in your lines, most of them broken, irregular. Our work then is to trace it back to its source, chase the riders back to the crimson palace."

Bosco frowns and mouths the word "shit," then tilts the cigar box for Ray to see the strings of cheap, plastic beads. He replaces the box and eases the drawer closed. In the corner of the room, a painted screen partially hides an iron bed and a chest of drawers. Bosco steps over and leans his hands against the chest of drawers. His shadow dips and angles against the opposite wall.

"Chase the riders? What the fuck are you talking about, Leo?" Ray says.

Leo lifts his hand to gesture, his rings flashing. "The riders are stray emotions, wants, unfulfilled dreams. They are sent out by the crimson palace—your heart." He smiles. "We're speaking metaphorically, friend."

Ray nods as if this makes some sense to him, and Bosco ducks behind the screen. Ray watches him in the mirror. Bosco slides open the top drawer.

Leo leans across the table, sending up wafts of cologne. His eyes are slate colored, bloodshot. He is no longer studying Ray's hand, only holding it. "What are yours?" he asks.

Ray draws back, tethered by his own hand. "What are my what?"

Bosco slowly lifts something out of the second drawer and sets it on top of the dresser. He looks back over his shoulder, catching Ray's eye.

"Your unfulfilled dreams, the empty areas of your existence," Leo says. He smiles like a cop, like he knows something. Ray closes his eyes, wanting this whole thing over with, wanting to be back on the barge, watching the water.

"Go on, Ray," Bosco says. Ray opens his eyes and Bosco is standing beside the screen, hands behind his back. Leo does not turn to look at him. Bosco grins. "Go ahead and tell old Leo about your so-called dream."

Ray feels the heat in his face.

"Yes, Ray," Leo says, "what is your so-called dream, as your friend puts it?"

Ray shakes his head. This is something he does not talk about. He only ever told Bosco because of a night of too many tequila shots and no moon, the river and the barge wrapped in nightfall, the generator out of gas, only the quiet and the drunken surges inside and his feet in the warm water, words spilling out into the darkness. And for the reason of their silent work together in the river hauling oysters out of the mud, thirty feet down, roped to each other, feeling their way through the murk of the river. Thinking of all that, loose and drunk, he let slip and knew right off how hollow it sounded, his dream of diving in the ocean, swimming through currents with tanks on his back, a kid wish he'd kept with him like some lucky penny left in a pocket and tarnished with age. But still he keeps it, fingering the notion, imagining it when he is driving his route and rain comes. Stuck on some back road, wipers burned out, waiting for the storm to pass, water washing sideways in ripples across his windshield, he will press his face to the glass and think of sharks and eels, of bright fish and coral reefs. He has never seen these things except on TV, which he knows is next to not seeing them at all, worse maybe, for how TV makes everything small and flat.

"Well, goddamn, Ray," Bosco had said that night. "Your truck's right there. Right *there*. Get in it and head south for twelve hours. You'll hit the damn ocean. Hell, if we could get the barge unstuck, we'd be there by breakfast."

Ray shook his head and shrugged, his awkwardness invisible in the darkness. "It ain't the ocean, really. The ocean is just a thing, like my head just picked it. I don't know."

"So you're all but dying to see the ocean but not really the ocean. Now we're making sense." Bosco threw a bottle out into the river.

Ray wanted to say then how after so much time the ocean meant nothing more than some new thing, how he wore the boredom of his thirty-eight years like a sickness, how his life ran past like the water past the barge—giving him only the trick of movement. He felt he was done with living, or it with him, and that apart from what he'd already been through—a handful of shit jobs, a year of marriage, a week in the county jail—nothing much else was left to happen.

"Give my word, Ray," Bosco said. "We'll get our asses on down to Biloxi as soon as oyster season's up."

Ray shrugged, pushed his bottle under the surface and let it sink.

Now Leo squeezes his hand and whispers. "You needn't cling to sadness, son. Tell me your dream."

"Yeah, tell him," Bosco says, and smirks. "Tell him about the ocean."

"The ocean?" Leo raises his eyebrows.

Ray's face flushes. "Just shut the fuck up, Bosco."

"You dream of leaving, of escape," Leo says, nodding. "Water represents birth, renewal, baptism."

"Don't talk about it," Ray says. He jerks his hand from Leo's grasp. "Bosco, keep your goddamn mouth closed."

Bosco shakes his head and smiles, then slowly withdraws his hands from behind his back and holds up to the light a large and imperfect diamond. He nods, grinning wildly.

Leo raises his hands in a gesture of mock surrender. "My young friend," he says. "You show up here, you pay me ten dollars. What is it you want?"

Bosco steps behind Leo, makes a gun with his thumb and finger, and points it at the back of Leo's head. They are like that for a moment—Leo awaiting Ray's answer, his hands still in the air, Bosco with his phantom gun. The seconds play out this pantomime of robbery, until the realization opens within Ray: They *could* do it. Bosco is right. They could.

"This is a two-way street," Leo says. "You come back when you decide how I can help you." Ray does not speak, his mind still held by that brief flash in Bosco's fingers. He looks again at Bosco, who hammers down his thumb trigger and mouths the word "pow." Bosco grins again, tips his head toward the door.

"I'll do that," Ray says, standing, shaking. "I will come back."

.   .   .

Early Friday morning, after his route, Ray drives out County
Road 10 and pulls over beside Sunshine Dairy. The windows of
the building reflect the dust-colored light of dawn. Ray thinks
of Leo inside, sleeping, the strung feathers twisting slightly in
the dark, the capping machines and cream separators below
him, the diamonds shining and hidden, their value hoarded
away. He sees it so clearly, Bosco yanking the .38 from his denim
coat, jamming the steel against the back of Leo's skull, the
blood and flesh and hair exploding like carp out of the river bottom. Ray watches the gray windows of Leo's apartment, his
mind drawing the stillness of that death from out of this stillness, the one before him now, lit pale orange as the sun rises
on the faint noise of radio static. As he watches, a light clicks
on and the drapes part. A wedge of Leo's face appears in the
gap between the curtains. Ray pushes back into his seat, guns
the engine, and spins out, his fingers shaking. By the time he
crosses into Clarendon, the town has started up again. Ray stops
at the Quik-Mart for cigarettes and beer and donuts, two car-
tons of chocolate milk for Bosco. Today is for oystering, and
Ray is relieved in this; beneath the river, there will be no talk of
killing.

The night before, after they left Leo's, it was all Bosco could
talk about, wound up like a kid on his way to the circus—
breathless, bouncing in the seat of the truck.

"Hey, look at this," he said, drawing the stolen diamond
from his pocket. The stone was milk white, irregularly shaped.

"Real smart," Ray said. "He's probably calling the cops right
now."

Bosco shook his head. "Never miss it. Had fifty of these if he
had one. An old Parcheesi box." He shook his head again.

"Think I'd find a better hiding place for my stash." Bosco nudged Ray. "I think I *will*."

"We don't even know that's a real diamond," Ray said, though looking, he knew.

Bosco gripped the stone and drew a long, thin scratch across the width of Ray's windshield.

"Now what do you say?" Bosco asked. "Could write the fucking Declaration of Independence if I wanted to."

Ray kept driving toward the river without speaking, as he drives now through the early morning. Traffic is heavy going the other way, the men in suits and ties headed into Berryville, the women putting on makeup in their rearview mirrors, coffee cups steaming their windshields. The scratch on his own windshield catches the morning sun, making tiny prisms, needles of colored light.

In the river along the barge, two of their antifreeze jugs bounce, pulling under the surface and then popping up again. They haul up catfish thrashing onto the deck. Bosco tries to club them with the butt of his .38, missing each time, the metal deck of the barge clanging. He grabs a fish to hold it down, and the dorsal fin pierces the palm of his hand.

"Shit *damn*," Bosco shouts. He falls back onto the deck, kicking the fish back into the river, still hooked to its line. His gun skitters across the barge.

"Can you think of any other ways to kill yourself?" Ray asks. Bosco sucks on his palm while Ray takes the gun, hauls up the antifreeze jug, lifts the fish into the air, and shoots it through the head. He unhooks the limp fish and tosses it to Bosco.

"See if you can skin it and get it in the cooler without losing a limb. Then we'll get the heater in the water."

Bosco grins, his mouth wet with his own blood. "Yessir, boss man."

Ray retrieves from the cabin their plastic bucket of weights, most of them old iron window sash weights, along with scraps of steel they found on the barge. He fills the front and back pockets of his jeans, and with a length of rope makes a belt of sash weights to tie around his waist. The second belt he makes for Bosco, who is still struggling with the pliers, trying to skin the catfish. It will go bad before he finishes. Now fifty pounds heavier, Ray takes a pint of bourbon from the fridge and drinks. The bottom of the river is always cold, even in August. Ray walks out and ties the weight belt to Bosco, then stuffs his pockets full of iron while Bosco wipes off his hands. He holds up the bottle so Bosco can drink, spilling some down his shirt front. Finally, he uncurls fifty feet of clothesline and cinches either end to their waists.

Bosco drinks again. "Let us not forget our tithes and offerings, brothers," he says. "When the Lord has delivered into our hands those goddamn diamonds, let us give back to Jesus."

Ray stiffens at the mention of the diamonds. For the whole day Bosco has been planning how they will have the diamonds cut and sold in Little Rock, and how they will spend the money—fast cars and stereos and guns. He talks as if their lives are fairy tales, already written.

"So it's blasphemy now," Ray says. "We're trying something new."

"Listen, bud, if God was of a mind to strike me down, he'd of gotten me twenty fuckups ago."

Ray unchains the water heater from the side of the barge and floats it around to the front. The river currents lift and push it, banging it against the barge. Ray thinks that if it hit hard enough, it could knock them off their shoal and into open water. They tie it off to one of the cleats on the barge, then grasp it on opposite sides, gripping it by its brass valves and pipe fittings. They draw deep breaths, readying themselves to strain against the weight of it. The old heater shell is lead-lined, industrial-size, nearly as heavy as a small car.

"All the way up," Ray says. "Nice big bubble for us." Words he repeats every time, a kind of incantation. They count three and lift the heater, the two of them grunting and spitting, until it is upright and flush against the surface of the water.

"Now," Ray says through his teeth, and they drop it, careful not to let it tip. They wait until it slips beneath the surface, thick rope coiling in after it. No bubble rises after the rope stops, and they know it has landed upright in the mud.

"We're good," Ray says. He draws five deep breaths, holds his clam rake tight to his chest, and jumps in, the weights in his clothes pulling him down. The rope around his waist tightens until he hears the muffled *sloosh* of Bosco jumping in after him. He has learned to keep his eyes open underwater, and watches overhead as the filtered light shifts from murky yellow to dull brown and then is gone almost completely. His feet settle on the bottom and he moves toward where he thinks the heater has landed, his boots sinking in, pulled downward. With his hands he finds the heater, and as his eyes adjust he can see it, faint white, slightly tilted. Ray gives two tugs on the rope and waits for Bosco to find him, hearing only the pounding of his heart in his ears. Three minutes he will last without a breath, the noise of his pulse like a clock reminding him. Bosco is there suddenly and they set to work, moving out from the heater like spokes from a hub, with or against the pull of the river. They rake the mud for oysters and clams, prying them out, saving them in burlap sacks tied to their belts. Later, sitting on the barge, they will sort them for size. Ray works quickly, his lungs feeling as though they, too, are weighted. His used-up air lets loose in quick, fat bursts as his muscles repeat their pattern—rake, dig, sack—like some song his body sings within itself. After twenty steps he turns back, lungs throbbing, the pulse of blood in the muscles of his face.

Ray is first beneath the heater, always, as Bosco seems able to hold his breath forever. He gives Ray a thumbs-up sign in the dark swirl of mud they have stirred. They lift the heater, and Bosco steadies it long enough for Ray to slide underneath and up in. Inside the heater is black as ink, the smelt full of musk and rot, the curved walls sweaty, slick with moss and algae. There is no water down as far as his knees. Ray gulps mouthfuls of the trapped air, talks to himself to hear a voice, breathes again, then raps his knuckles on the wall and listens for the sound of Bosco lifting the heater for him.

For half a minute there is no sound, and Ray raps the wall again. "Dammit, Bosco," he yells. He pushes up, without enough leverage to budge the heater. This prank is one that Bosco never tires of, one he will pull on Ray a couple times a week.

"Okay, fine," Ray shouts. "Stay out there and drown your sorry ass."

Finally there comes the squeak of Bosco's hands searching for a grip, then the suck of mud at the bottom. Ray takes one last deep breath and squirms out through the gap. He holds the heater for Bosco to go inside. Looming up in Ray's face, Bosco grins and gives another thumbs-up, then disappears. They work this way for over an hour, raking the spokes, filling their bags, taking their turns inside the heater. At the end of their work they turn the hot water valve at the top of the heater and let it fill, then climb the heater's rope back up to the barge, the weight belts and oyster bags hanging down, pulling at them.

They stand dripping on the deck of the barge, tossing off their weights.

"Had you that time," Bosco says, panting. "You thought I'd got washed away."

"Hell, yes, you fooled me. About twice as much as three days ago when you pulled the same trick."

"Well, this is near about the last time we have to dig oysters out of the shit. After we get those diamonds."

Ray nods, wipes mud from his face.

"Tell me this right now, Bosco. You gonna put the gun against his head? Pull the trigger? Stand there with pieces of Leo's brain down your shirt, blood on your hands, and then go digging through his shit? You can do all that?"

"Hell, Ray, you ever seen me handle a gun? I mean it—"

Ray shoves him hard against his good shoulder, staggering him. Bosco looks stung, his mouth open, dark water running in thin lines across his face.

"No more of your bullshit," Ray says. "Tell me here and now. You need that money or you might die." Ray lightly taps Bosco's other shoulder, where the pain is, where the cancer has been. "No bullshit, just listen. I ain't dying, but I ain't afraid of good money, either. So you tell me, Bosco. A gun in your hand, you raise it up, you fire into Leo's head. You shatter his skull. More blood than you've seen in your life. Think about that, Bosco, and tell me. You going to be able to do it?"

They stand facing each other, the puddles around their feet joining. Bosco's mouth works, his eyes dart to the side. He will not look at Ray.

"Go on. You say the word, and we'll dump these fucking oysters back in the river and head over right now. Got your gun loaded? Just say."

Bosco looks off toward the water curling past the edge of the barge. His eyes well up, his face flushed. He slowly shakes his head, not speaking.

Ray points a finger at him. "That's it, then, understand? Not another goddamn word about it."

They use up the afternoon parked at the juncture of Highways 45 and 19, in the shade of a tree, selling the oysters out of a cooler in the back of Ray's pickup. They sell mostly to people from town headed back to their country houses, men with their ties loosened, women in convertibles with the tops up. Ray uses a scale he made to weigh more than true by taking it apart and stretching the spring. They charge six dollars a pound, a dollar cheaper than IGA.

When they have sold out or when what is left has gone bad, the shells opening, they will head into town, stopping at the liquor store on the way. By the time they get where they are going—usually the Lightbulb Club or the Barbary Coast—they are half-drunk on bourbon. Today, though, Ray eases off a little, steering toward the fire station on River Road, for what he calls the best deal in town, all-you-can-eat fried chicken and

barbecue for four dollars, with slaw and biscuits and lemonade
on the side.

"Every damn body and their seven kids will be there," Bosco
says. "Ain't worth it."

"It's worth it," Ray tells him. "I'm sick of hauling dinner out
of that shithole river. Sick of all of it."

"Plus, there won't be no women there," Bosco says. "Just
housewives." He wipes his nose on his sleeve.

Ray nods, pleased that Bosco has found something to pout
over, to distract him from the diamonds. He has not mentioned
them since that morning. All afternoon, in the hot shade of the
tree, Ray has seen Leo alone in his apartment, seen the small
swirl of the feathers, has heard Leo's breath in the quiet room.
He thinks of the cancer growing inside Bosco's shoulder, cells
gone wrong and dark, growing there maybe even now, as Bosco
drinks and wipes his mouth. He thinks of himself, shucking off
his thirty-eight years like oyster shells. It would be two lives for
one, he thinks. Two for one.

At the firehouse the men in their blue uniforms sweat over
gas grills while the wind whips paper plates and napkins off the
picnic tables and around the yard. Mothers and fathers sit on
blankets spread across the grass. The bigger kids hurl water balloons at one another while the little kids crowd around a fat,
panting dalmatian—Sparky—who shows the kids how to stop,
drop, and roll, put through his paces by a short fireman with a
blond mustache.

The man taking money sits at a card table in the driveway.
Ray pays for both of them and waits for his change.

"You boys aren't drunk, are you?" the man says. He gives
them a smile with no humor in it. The man wants to find some

excuse to keep them out, Ray thinks. Two river rats fucking up his nice family gathering.

"Not drunk," Rays says. "Just hungry as hell." Bosco laughs.

They stand in line for chicken and barbecue, cole slaw, biscuits, peach cobbler, and lemonade. Both pile their plates so high that some of the food teeters off into the grass. Bosco pulls his pint of bourbon from his pocket and refills their half-emptied lemonade cups. When they finish, Ray feels doubly drunk, from the whiskey and from his overly fed stomach. He eats one last biscuit, not from hunger but just for the excess of it, sloshing it around in his mouth with a gulp of the spiked lemonade. He can't remember when he felt this happy, eating the way he did as a kid visiting his grandparents in Hot Springs, going a night without eating carp and mudfish from out of the dirty river and drinking half-warmed beer. Soon it will be fall again, oyster season over and back to little money, just what he makes from his route and whatever he and Bosco can throw together in the way of odd jobs. Last year it was helping businesses downtown string up their Christmas lights for four bucks an hour. For a man his age, nothing more than sympathy work.

He looks over at Bosco, who is still chewing and swallowing, bobbing his head in time with the bluegrass music that spills out of the loudspeaker mounted on the side of the firehouse. Every so often the music is interrupted by the crackle and chirp of the dispatcher radioing the sheriff's deputies. A couple of the young parents dance in a ring around their children, who laugh and giggle in the middle. Ray takes the bottle from Bosco and pours over the ice in his cup. He swallows, hardly tasting it now, his happiness climbing like some balloon he's released. He gets up and starts dancing, too, Bosco tugging on his pant leg, telling him to sit down. He wanders around the yard, stepping on blankets, thinking how strange it is that all these people—his age, many of them, or younger—have ended up this way. They have nice shining cars, nice shining houses, nice shining jobs.

"Nice shining lives," Ray says aloud, not aware until he's said it that he has been thinking this. He laughs at the idea that these people have got where they are by following some simple plan, going to school, meeting the right people. That's all fine. His real question is how they knew from the start that there was supposed to *be* a plan, how did they know to move in some direction and not another? He stops now at the outside edge of a ring of children, a new group gathered around to watch Sparky go through his paces. He can see their polished lives laid out before them. He remembers teachers, principals, counselors from high school, two decades past now, telling him he needed direction. He can hear them saying it, see their faces. How was he to know that they only meant that his life would end up somewhere, and that automatic pilot brought you down low to stay? *I have direction,* he thinks, though the children turning to look at him tells him that he must be talking out loud again. His direction is down, the bottom of the river, then back to where he started, ready the next day to go down again. Down, down, Bosco behind or below him, tethered to him, the two ends of some finite thing, always down.

Sparky catches a Milk-bone tossed by the fireman. The dog wags his tail and the children clap. For a better view, Ray lifts himself onto the platform of the ladder truck parked in the driveway, its doors open for display, the ladder extended into the air.

"Always tell Mom and Dad to test those smoke detectors," the fireman says. Sparky nods and the children laugh.

"Have a plan for getting out," the fireman says.

A plan. For getting out. The words fill Ray's mouth as he repeats them, resonate at the bottom of his cup as he drinks, burn at the back of his throat. The children stare up at him, the fireman glares. He smiles at them. We have our plan, he wants to tell them. He and Bosco. For getting out. For getting off the bottom of the river. *Leo . . . gun . . . Parcheesi box . . . diamonds.* Ray tries to shake the idea from his head. Maybe they are done with it, and Bosco won't pull anymore. Maybe Ray's speech earlier has ended it, planting them forever at the river bottom.

"Why do you think we bring Sparky to the fires?" the fireman asks. Ray can tell this is the setup for some cornball joke.

"I know," Ray says, and they all turn toward him, sudden as a school of fish. "He pisses on it when the rest of you fuckers get wrung out."

The fireman's face darkens. "I think you need to get on home now, buddy, sleep it off."

Ray smiles. "I ain't your fucking buddy."

The fireman points his finger, raises his voice. "Now you listen—"

Ray whistles and snaps his fingers. "Here, boy. C'mon, boy." Sparky jumps up and trots in Ray's direction, the show only half over. The children look around, confused. Bosco is there suddenly, calling for Ray to come down off the truck. Ray likes this, the fireman flustered, everything mixed up. He has spoiled the plan. He sees this as the core of living in this world: plans made or not made, plans messed up. They have a plan for getting out and will not use it if Bosco will not talk about it, if Bosco will let himself die quietly instead.

"I think we're done here, Ray," Bosco says, pulling at his pant leg. Ray yanks loose from his grip and steps up on the ladder. He climbs about twenty feet and some of the children clap, thinking this is part of the show.

"What do you think you're doing?" the fireman yells. Sparky barks.

"Hey, Bosco," Ray shouts down, his tongue thick in his mouth. "What's your plan for next spring? What say we dive down to the river bottom, rake around in the shit, then do it again the next day, then a thousand more times after that."

Bosco shrugs. "Okay."

Ray climbs farther up the ladder, feeling it sway under him. He can see the air conditioners on top of the firehouse, and, in the distance, a corner of the river. Other firemen leave their posts at the gas grills and trot over to surround the back of the truck. Ray turns and sits on the rung.

"Come down from there now," a fireman shouts. "We can't be responsible for your safety. The outriggers aren't extended."

"Careful, Bosco," Ray says. "You might want to check your calendar, make double sure about next spring." He laughs at his joke, then stands and looks a hundred feet up at the top of the ladder. He thinks of climbing all the way up, then decides against it. Just more up and down, going nowhere.

"I'm sure, Ray," Bosco says, sober with his embarrassment.

Ray climbs down to the platform, then jumps to the pavement. The firemen tell him to get lost before they call the sheriff, and some of the children start clapping again.

"Okay, then," he tells Bosco. "We're set."

. . .

That night Ray makes an excuse of wanting tequila, which means a ride to the liquor store in Berryville, down the highway past Leo's place. Ray wants to feel the pull of the dairy, the thin stretch of lawn and plaster wall separating them from that other life. He wants to know if it is enough to draw murder from them. He thinks of little else as they ride into the early gray of night, the noise of I-40 rising on the near horizon. As they pass Leo's, the dairy is dark, Bosco is punching the buttons on Ray's radio, complaining that there are no decent rock 'n' roll stations. In Berryville they buy their tequila, drinking as they head back toward Clarendon. All along the road are the mashed bodies of frogs, which appear on the highways in the late part of summer, signaling its end.

Ray takes a long swig, the tequila a burning rope through him. As they pass the dairy again he taps the brakes, slowing. Yellow light from Leo's window angles across the yard and gravel driveway. His curtains are open, a box fan on the windowsill. Leo stands shirtless in front of it. Faint music finds its way to the open window of Ray's truck.

Ray passes the bottle to Bosco. He can feel the tequila inside him, an invisible thumb pushing him down. "There it is," he says.

"There what is?" Bosco drinks, some of it spilling down his shirt. He wipes his mouth on his sleeve.

"Leo's place, what do you think I mean?"

"He's standing right there, probably giving himself a massage." Bosco smiles, wiping his shirtfront. He is so thin now, wasting away inside his clothes.

"Bet he's planning how to spend his money," Ray says. He cuts his eyes at Bosco, then looks at the slice of road lit by his headlights.

"He *don't* spend it, that's the damn waste of the whole thing. If that was me, I would . . . I don't know, find something to spend it on. I'd buy stuff." He sniffs, scratches at his tooth with a fingernail. Ray hits the gas and watches in the rearview as the yellow light recedes. They ride in silence, slowly killing the bottle.

"You were right on what you said," Bosco finally says. It is fully dark now, Ray cannot see his face.

"Right on what?"

"On not being able to do Leo the way we said. You were one hundred percent on that one. Just not in me to pull that trigger."

Ray takes a long swallow, warmth and relief mixing inside him. Tomorrow is for oysters, he thinks. A few dollars in their pockets.

Near the river bridge they see the lights from downtown reflected, the fluorescent glow off the Methodist church spire, the faint glow of their trotline jugs. The barge is farther down, hidden in shadow. Later, they sit on the couch at the edge of the barge, drinking down toward the end of the bottle, chasing it with beer, drinking for hours. It is the way it was before Bosco's cancer, when Ray visited only on weekends. They talk of going into the Barbary Coast, trying to lure some women back to the barge. Bosco is happy, talking about game shows, asking Ray to name the top five things you buy at the grocery store. When the mosquitoes get bad, Bosco hauls out a quart jar of citronella oil and they wipe their arms and faces with it. The river washes around them. Their antifreeze jugs bob in the dark.

"You're a different story," Bosco says, out of the dark. He smokes, the orange of his cigarette moving.

"What are you talking about, Bosco?"

"I mean, you could do it. To Leo. You're the one."

Ray tightens his hands on his beer bottle.

"You're drunk as hell, Bosco." His own drunkenness threatens to push him through the floor of the barge, down into the river bottom.

"Yeah, but I know you, Ray. You told me what you did today because you know me, and now I'm telling you because I know you just the same. You could kill Leo."

Ray's hands shake. "Don't talk about this shit anymore, Bosco. We're done with it."

"After we finished, you know what? I bet you'd say it was the easiest thing you'd ever done," Bosco says. For a moment, Ray thinks of shinnying across to his truck, starting it, leaving all this behind. But without Ray, Bosco would not be capable even of diving in the river for oysters, of catching carp. He would be lost. Ray picks up the .38, hefting it, letting his fingers curl around it. He clicks the safety off and on and off and on.

Bosco coughs and winces, rubs his shoulder. The gas lantern hisses at his feet. "I bet you already made plans for your half. Of course you oughta get more than half, you pull the trigger. I mean, that's only f—"

"Shut your goddamn mouth, Bosco." Rays raises the .38 to Bosco's head, clicks the safety off, pulls back the hammer.

Bosco smiles, looks at him. "Right now? You're just proving my point." Ray lets the hammer down and eases the safety back on. For a minute, neither of them speak.

"And you better listen," Bosco says, whispering above the sound of the water. "Without that money, Ray, I'll die. You ever stop and think about that?" He flicks his cigarette into the river, then pulls the diamond from his pants pocket and taps it nervously on the wooden arm of the couch. Ray looks at him, his face lit faintly by the light of early dawn, the grayness of disease on him like a second skin.

"You're talking about a man's life," Ray says. Already the town is waking up, cars moving across the bridge.

"You're goddamn right we are," he says. Bosco wipes his mouth with his fingers, his hand shaking. The diamond glistens dully in his fingers.

Ray shakes his head. "We're done with it, Bosco."

"No we ain't," Bosco says. "You won't let me die, Ray. You won't."

Rays pushes himself up, stretches. "We should get this heater in the water." He has not slept, is still full of tequila and beer. He feels heavy, weighted down. He thinks of the cancer, thinks of it growing, cell by cell, in Bosco's shoulder.

"You'd just better hear me, Ray," Bosco says, slipping the diamond back in his pocket, "because I ain't finished. I ain't gonna finish."

Ray pretends to ignore him. He grabs the water heater and struggles with it alone until Bosco finally helps. They muscle it up, then stop to rest, breathing together, Bosco holding his chest with one hand.

"Everything is easy, Ray," Bosco says. "I'll load the gun and talk us inside. I swear I will. Hell, I'll drive if you want me to. Ray . . . you know you will."

Ray steadies the heater, leveling it on the water. "Nice big bubble for us," he says without thinking. He can feel Bosco staring at him. They release the heater, then wait to make sure their bubble does not escape and rise to the surface.

"We're good," Rays says. They silently pass the bag of weights, filling their pockets, stringing their belts. Ray uncurls the clothesline to tether them together.

They stand at the edge of the barge. Bosco grins. "Last time we'll have to—" he starts to say, before Ray leaps into the river, sinking fast, moved by the current. He feels the rope tighten, Bosco pulled in behind him. He settles in the gravel and mud. The water is clearer than usual, a light, murky gold. He walks until the heater looms up in his vision, white and blurry. He gives the two quick tugs on the rope and Bosco soon finds him. They work out from the heater in their long spokes. It is slow today, only a few oysters under their rakes. When it is time they lift the heater and Bosco strains, holding it while Ray slips underneath. The darkness of it always startles him, like instant blindness. He hears himself pant for breath, runs his fingers around the mossy sides. He holds his head in his hands, squeezes, breathes.

Ray taps the side of the heater and Bosco lifts it to let him out. Ray takes it from him to allow Bosco inside. Just before he slips under, Bosco holds up the diamond and gives Ray a thumbs-up. His face is drawn, desperate, searching Ray's eyes. He slips down and in. Without the money he will die, and without Ray he will not have the money. He believes in everything that Ray is to him, just as he believes that bullshit and stupid jokes are equal to cancer, that killing is some easy thing. He pulls his faith from TV shows. They are moving toward the things he believes in now, he is pulling Ray toward them, toward the explosion of brain and hair and blood, toward the shining box of diamonds. In the dark water and the throbbing of his lungs the scene repeats itself like memory. Bosco taps the side of the heater. He will reemerge, his eyes panicked and full of death. The taps on the heater grow louder—sharper and more distinct—and Ray realizes that Bosco is tapping with the diamond. The clicks resonate like gunshots through some distant wall, mixed in the noise of his pulse in his ears, of the slow push of water. He shakes his head, his lungs aching already, too soon, way before his time in the heater. His chest burns, the taps coming in sharp ripples of sound as his fingers work at the knotted rope around his waist, at the belt of weights holding him down. He unties them and rises slightly, Bosco's voice shouting from a thousand miles away as Ray twists the hot water valve atop the heater, letting in the water, the bubbles rising fat and bright, moving upward as the taps of the diamond quicken and then slow, as Ray gives himself to the current, following the bubbles, his lungs strained to bursting, his eyes held by a patch of greasy light above him. He rises, flailing through moments, as if all he could know of what would come next and next were held above him always, just beyond reach, in a layer of thin white air.

About the Author

BRAD BARKLEY, a native of North Carolina, is the author of two novels, *Alison's Automotive Repair Manual*, which was a Book Sense 76 choice, and *Money, Love*, which was a Barnes & Noble Discover Great New Writers selection and a Book Sense 76 choice. *Money, Love* was named one of the best books of 2000 by the *Washington Post* and *Library Journal*. *Book* magazine named Barkley as one of their Newcomers of 2002: Breakthrough Writers You Need to Know. His short fiction has appeared in over two dozen publications, including *USA Today*, the *Raleigh News & Observer*, the *Southern Review*, the *Georgia Review*, the *Oxford American*, the *Greensboro Review*, *Glimmer Train*, *Book* magazine, and the *Virginia Quarterly Review*, which has twice awarded him the Emily Balch Prize for Best Fiction. He has twice been nominated for the Pushcart Prize, once earning Special Mention, and was short-listed in *Best American Short Stories, 1997*, and again in 2002. His work is anthologized in *New Stories from the South: The Year's Best, 2002*. He has won four Individual Artist Awards from the Maryland State Arts Council, and a Creative Writing Fellowship from the National Endowment for the Arts. Brad Barkley teaches creative writing at Frostburg State University. He lives in western Maryland with his wife, Mary, and two children.